Christmas Undercover

JO LEIGH

First published in Great Britain 2006
Silhouette Books, Eton House, 18-24 Paradise Road, Richmond, Surrey TW9 1SR

ISBN-13: 978 0 373 40271 7
ISBN-10: 0 373 40271 6

46-1106

Printed and bound in Spain
by Litografia Rosés S.A., Barcelona

JO LEIGH

lives way the heck up on a mountain in Utah with her own personal hero and her many chipmunk friends. She loves to hear from readers at www.joleigh.com.

CAST OF CHARACTERS

Max Travis—When all the evidence points to him as a cold-blooded killer, Jade is his last and only hope.

Jade Parker—In order to save her father's reputation, must she destroy the man she loves?

Senator William Parker—His terrible secrets have put his daughter in the crosshairs of a killer.

CJ Harris—With billions at stake, he'll stop at nothing—including murder—to get what he wants.

Joseph Retik—He only has one objective: to get rid of anyone in the way.

Chapter One

Pain woke him. A sharp poke in the ribs. Max Travis groaned as he struggled to open his eyes. Cold, biting cold, made his movements as stiff as the slab of rock beneath him.

"You can't sleep here." A cop, bundled in a heavy winter coat, stood scowling above him.

Max blinked, dizziness making it hard to focus, disorientation making it impossible to think. "Where am I?"

"On my beat, so get your ass up and out of here. I don't care where you go, but you can't stay here."

Max put his elbow on the cold stone and pushed himself into a sitting position. Everything ached, and when he rubbed his eyes he found ice crystals on his lashes. He cursed as he fought to get his bearings, to figure out what the hell was going on.

The cop gave him one more jab in the side with his nightstick. "The soup kitchen is on Fourth. Don't let me find you out here again."

Max didn't bother with a response. He had other things to worry about. Like the fact that he could barely move his fingers. That he had no idea where he was, or how he'd gotten here. The last thing he could remember was the bar last night. He'd had a drink with a couple of guys from the paper. Which would have explained things, except, he'd been drinking soda. He hadn't touched booze for over six months.

He shifted on what he saw was marble. Marble? He turned, the motion making him groan, and not a little nauseous. Behind him, Abraham Lincoln sat impervious to the weather. The Lincoln Memorial? What the…?

He stood up too quickly and had to grab the corner of the bench. All he could manage were a few deep breaths, the cold hurting his lungs. What the hell had happened to him? His head pounded with pain so intense he couldn't think at all. It helped to focus on his scratchy throat. What he wouldn't do for a bottle or ten of aspirin.

When he opened his eyes, the cop had gone and the tourists, drawn to the Lincoln statue, gave him a wide berth. If he looked like he felt, he didn't blame them.

He didn't think he was going to vomit, but he moved slowly nonetheless, turning toward the street. His car was nowhere in sight, which wasn't surprising. What did surprise him was that his wallet was still in his pocket, along with his credit cards, driver's license and thirteen dollars. So were his keys.

It was Monday. At least he hoped it was. He was supposed to meet his friend and colleague Peter Shelby at the café, then go in to work to face J.G. He cursed, scaring an Asian woman walking her baby. It occurred to him that he still had his watch. Four past seven. Monday. So it was only the one night he couldn't account for.

Again, he thought about the bar. He'd ordered a soda, even though Jeremy had called him a little girl. It hadn't bothered him. Not ordering his favorite scotch had, but that was between him and his maker. Whom he'd clearly almost met overnight.

Max headed toward Twenty-third street. He could catch a cab there and go back to the bar, see if his car was still parked around the corner. Then he'd call Pete, cancel the breakfast chat. He had two hours to get his act together before seeing his boss, and he'd need an hour of that for a shower.

As he walked, his head cleared. It didn't feel a whole lot better, but his thoughts clarified a little. Enough to figure out that he'd been slipped a Mickey. Something damn strong to have wiped everything after it right off the slate.

Why? Who?

The only thing he could think of was Geotech. The woman. The redhead. She'd come on to him, using a fine set of double D's and the most incredible red lips, and he'd been putty in her hands. Ready to swim great oceans, or at the very least buy her dinner.

And then, nothing. No memories until the cop had jabbed him. A royal headache, the taste of many pairs of army boots in his mouth, and a terrible feeling that his investigation into Senator William Parker and Geotech had gone from the suspect to the criminal. He wasn't just close to the truth, he was right on ground zero.

HIS CAR was still in front of the Guardian bar, the engine so cold it took five minutes to warm it up enough to turn on the heater. His gloves sat on the dashboard. He usually kept them in his coat pocket but last night he hadn't bothered. His plan had been to hoist a few, get an order of the famous chili fries, then get his ass home.

He headed there now, creeping through the slow D.C. morning traffic. He'd left his cell phone at the house along with his laptop. Even if whoever had drugged him had gotten into his apartment and stolen his computer, they wouldn't find much. He was too careful for that. Everything was encrypted, and the pertinent data was kept on separate disks, hidden behind the wall in his bathroom.

He thought again about the redhead. He'd left her for a few minutes to hit the head, that's when she must have doctored his drink. Probably one of the date-rape drugs, although he felt pretty sure her intent hadn't been to have her way with him. So what was her goal? Why knock him out and leave him on a public bench? Why not kill him, if they wanted the story stopped? Why not beat the crap out of him in the way of thugs everywhere, warning him to back the hell off?

He found a decent parking spot a block away from his apartment. He locked the car, shivering in the still freezing air. It took him awhile to actually get to his building, the five-story box that was the essence of tenement living. He didn't give a damn. No one bothered him here, he was close to work, close to the center of life in D.C.

The elevator ride with all the lurching and grumbling was a quiet nightmare, and then it was all he could do not to bump the walls in his hallway as he made it to his door. It took him a minute to fish his keys out of his pocket. As he pushed the key into the lock, the door swung open. "Damn."

He suddenly felt both better and worse. His stomach rose into his throat, but his mind was horribly clear. If he had an ounce of smarts he would get the hell out, call the police. For all he knew someone was inside, ready to finish what the drugs had started. But he'd never been smart. He listened, heard nothing, then took a step inside. That's when he saw the body. Despite the big winter coat, he recognized the dead man instantly. He'd known him all his life.

"Werner?" he whispered, knowing there would be no answer. The old man lay on his back, his coat soaked with blood, an unnatural pallor to his face. Trying to avoid the wide pool of coagulating blood, Max knelt near the body and put his hand to the cold neck, but could feel no pulse.

Max stood slowly. The plan wasn't all that sophisticated. Wipe his memory with drugs, give him no alibi. Or maybe they wanted him to come home and pass out with Werner Edwards dead in his living room. A variation on a theme—instead of simply beating him up to warn him off, kill the man with the real skinny and pin it on Max. If that was what they had in mind....

His next thought was answered by the sound of approaching sirens. Someone was watching his place, all right. Waiting for him to get home. He only had a few minutes.

With a clarity that was pure fear, he went to the

bedroom and grabbed his laptop, the power cord, his cell phone. In the bathroom, he moved aside the false brick and took out his baggie full of disks. Then he stuffed some clean socks, his toothbrush, and a few other personal items into his duffle bag.

He moved hurriedly back to the living room and stood by the front door, trying to narrow his thinking to the basics. Was there anything else he might need soon? He'd have to head straight for the bank and get as much cash as possible. Beyond that…

Beyond that would have to wait. The sirens were too damn close.

"Goodbye, Werner." Max looked sadly at his elder friend. "Damn, I'm sorry." He closed the door and ran past the elevator to the stairway.

AT FOUR in the afternoon, in mid-December, the Senate Office Building was already lit up. The view from the fourth floor offices of the Honorable Senator William Parker granted Jade Parker a terrific view of the gridlocked traffic in the streets below. She watched impassively as behind her, her father attempted to exercise his considerable persuasive skills on her, with marginal success.

"Please, Jade. If you don't do this for me, who will?"

Jade turned from the baleful view of dirty snow and snarled traffic and looked the senator straight in the eye. "Why not Gertie, Dad? All the other senators have their secretaries do their Christmas shopping. I'm your executive assistant, for God's sake."

Her father sighed as he closed the distance between them, raised his hands to put them on her shoulders but thought better of it. "C'mon, honey. Do you really think I should leave it to Gertie to decide what the ambassador from Germany would like? Remember what she bought the president for his birthday?"

Jade winced as she thought about the president's expression when he'd opened up the gorgeously wrapped present. Being the consummate politician, he'd smiled, said he really liked the sweater, but even she, who hardly ever saw the man except on television, could tell he'd been appalled. With reason. But still.... "Do you suppose the ambassador celebrates Christmas at home? You're just asking me because you don't want to think about it." She folded her arms across her breasts and turned back to the window.

She could see his frown in the reflection as he moved closer. So big and solid, his white hair a little messy, his silk tie slightly crooked, he looked as tired as she'd ever seen him. She almost stepped away when he wrapped his arms around her. "What is it, Jade? This isn't like you."

She stiffened, then relaxed into the comfort of his arms, letting her head lay back against his shoulder. "I don't know, Dad. Finals, maybe. I keep thinking about Mom. I don't know."

He squeezed her lightly. "I miss her, too. That first Christmas after she died..."

Jade turned, gently moving out of his embrace. "I'm sorry, Dad. I didn't mean to—"

"That's okay. It's okay." He patted her awkwardly. "Even after three years, it still seems like yesterday."

They stood that way for a moment, each wrapped

in their own memories. Jade stepped away, walked over to his desk and stared at his in-basket without focusing. "No, I'm sorry I said anything. That's not the problem. None of that stuff is. I know you don't want to hear it, but dammit, I'm still being followed. I'm sure of it."

The senator walked over to her, his face, so familiar to millions of Americans, a study in concern. "The detective said—"

"The detective," she said, angry all over again. "I know he's supposed to be some kind of supersleuth, but he couldn't have been sleuthing very diligently. The man had the audacity to suggest it was all in my head. I know it isn't."

"I believe you. I'll get on the phone, talk to the head of the secret service. We'll have someone new on the case first thing in the morning. I won't let anything happen to you."

She picked up a snow globe of the U.S. Capitol, shaking it to mimic the weather outside. "I don't know. Maybe it is nothing."

The senator wasn't amused. "I don't believe that any more than you do. I'll take care of it. I promise." He folded his arms across his broad chest. "I've got a couple of hours of work left here, then that dinner with Jeffries. Why don't you take off now. Go home. Maybe what you need is a quiet evening by the fire. Get a good night's sleep."

Jade kissed him on the cheek. "It's a deal. But tell you what. I'll stop at the Arlington Fashion Center Mall and get a head start on the shopping. From that list you slipped into my purse, it's going to take me 'til next Christmas to get it all done."

"Why don't you wait until tomorrow, when we have someone we can trust watching your back."

"I'll be careful. I promise."

"The presents aren't that important."

She smiled, even though the thought of battling the crowds made her want to buy herself a quick trip to Jamaica. "Right. Maybe next year we'll find a professional shopper, huh?"

"It's a deal."

She got her purse from beside the wing chair, then pulled her coat from the rack. With a wave, she left the office and headed out to the mall, feeling better already that by tomorrow she'd have someone competent on her case.

JADE'S USUAL aggressiveness proved to be of marginal use in the crowded confines of the mall. In her heavy coat, clutching her purse tightly to her chest so pickpockets wouldn't get into it, she pushed her way through the throngs of Christmas shoppers.

She briefly considered stopping in at The Coffee Beanery for a latte, but one look at the people packed in like sardines and she changed her mind.

Besides, that feeling was back. The one that made the small hairs at the back of her neck stand up. Several times she'd stopped, letting the crowds wash around her, and tried to catch a familiar reflection in the shop window. Or at least the same face twice. It never happened. Maybe she was nuts.

She shrugged it off and focused on some serious shopping. Just like last year, it was easier to buy for those people who were on the periphery of her father's life, like the ambassador from Germany. The closer the circle got, the more personal the gift had to be, which was no piece of cake considering the disparity of the people involved.

She ended up finding her salvation at Hammacher Schlemmer, picking up a dozen tiny CD stereo systems, highly stylized, that could fit on any bookshelf. She also bought several back massagers, three facial saunas, and a couple of radio-controlled cars for her father's more emotionally stunted friends. The real bonus about the store was that they would deliver the entire purchase to the Senate office, where she could deal with the wrapping, cards and mailing at her leisure.

She had to schlep all the other packages though, and as they piled up, she grew less careful about checking reflections. By the time she got into Saks, she was more concerned with juggling bags and credit cards and not being poked, prodded or stepped on by the other harried shoppers.

As she signed for a jeweled cigar cutter, she glanced at her watch. She'd been in the mall for nearly two hours. Enough. She'd had it for tonight. In fact, she'd had it with malls. She'd do the rest of her shopping online.

There'd been a time when Christmas shopping had been fun, but that was when her mother had come with her. Jade headed toward the mall exit, thinking about that last Christmas—

A thought stopped her so sharply, the man behind her stepped on her heel. She heard his low curse, but she didn't care. The feeling she'd been having this week. Could it possibly be memories of her mother?

Too pragmatic to believe in ghosts or spirits, Jade

did believe that the mind was a powerful, mysterious thing. That the subconscious could play mighty tricks on the conscious. It was all too possible that she missed her mother so much that she'd conjured up the feeling of being watched. Although she'd ascribed fear to the experience, now that she understood it, that could change. She could gain comfort, instead.

She reshuffled the bags in her arms and continued toward the parking lot, wrestling with this new idea. Wondering if she should look up Doctor Frankle. She'd been a good therapist, not too heavy-handed, definitely not Freudian. Jade had seen her for eight months, after a terrible breakup and while deciding about getting her Ph.D. At the end of their time together, Jade had felt better, stronger. It wouldn't hurt to go for that feeling again.

As she exited the wide glass doors, she noticed two different Santas, complete with bells and donation buckets in front of them. Since she gave at the office and had no desire to disrupt the carefully constructed conglomerate of packages in her arms, she headed up the middle, eyes straight ahead.

She passed the gauntlet unscathed and made it to the massive parking lot without dislodging so much as a ribbon. Unfortunately, she'd parked in what felt like another county, and her right arm was already feeling numb.

The only good thing about parking so far in the hinterlands was the relative quiet. She'd never cared for crowds, and with all that was on her mind, they'd been particularly annoying in the mall. All she had to think about now was negotiating the traffic home.

Then it would be a roaring fire, sinfully buttered popcorn and movies, movies, movies.

Too bad her father had that dinner. It would have been nice to have a quiet evening with him, although he never did make it through the movies. He always talked about watching, but nothing held his attention. Not for two hours, that was for sure. Halfway through, he'd make up some excuse, like getting a drink, checking something from the office or even going to the bathroom. He always promised to come right back, but he never did. She'd stopped trying to change his ways.

He'd been like that forever, his fertile mind filled with his duties, his constituents, his campaigns. She couldn't blame him. He was definitely playing in the big leagues, and she realized it was a lot to ask him to relax, but she couldn't help her worry.

Ever since her mother died, he'd been running himself ragged. He worked impossible hours and ate horribly. The only reason he wasn't big as a horse was that he walked every day, mostly on the Hill. But still, his color wasn't good, and his hair, always his pride and joy, was thinning and dull. She'd begged him to get a full physical, but he kept putting it off.

That's what he could get her for Christmas. The thought of losing him, too, was entirely too much to bear, and she would manipulate his emotions mercilessly until he gave in.

She saw her car, finally, just a few aisles away. Rounding a pylon, she practically ran into a third Santa Claus. She gasped, almost losing her armload from the surprise. She stepped to her right just as he stepped to his left. Her smile died on her lips, however, when she looked more carefully at his face.

He stared at her with intense, bloodshot eyes, and his expression was anything but jovial. Her heart kicked into double-time as she realized he wasn't just another store Santa.

"Ms. Parker," he said.

That did it. How did he know her name? She looked to her right, her left, but there was no one nearby. Someone had to be around, for God's sake.

"Please, don't be scared, I just want to talk to you."

She checked to her left once more, tried to feint to her right. But his hand caught her arm, and his grip held her firm. She opened her mouth to scream, but the move came too late. His hand, thick, clammy, covered her mouth, the hand on her arm pulling her farther into the recesses of the garage.

She struggled against him, but he kept maneuvering her past cars, toward her SUV. God, he knew her car! She hadn't been crazy, or nostalgic for her mother. This maniac had been following her, stalking her, and now...

She remembered in a vivid flash the most serious admonition given to every woman: don't let the abductor get you into the car. The chances of surviving were minimal once he got you away from people, from crowds.

She kicked his leg, and his grunt let her know she'd made an impact, but it wasn't enough. His grip didn't loosen. In fact, his hand tightened brutally.

They got to the SUV and she heard something behind her, a car door closing. She tried to twist around, but he pushed up against her back, his warm breath and scratchy white beard tickling her neck.

"Don't make a sound," he whispered. "I won't hurt you as long as you stay quiet. I'm going to take my hand away from your mouth. I have a gun, and I have nothing to lose by shooting you."

A gun. Oh, God. She was going to die. She thought of the mace in her purse, and it might have been on the moon for all the help it did her. She should have just dropped her packages and run at the first hint of trouble, but she'd clung to the stupid gifts as if they mattered.

As promised, his hand moved from her mouth, and just as she was about to scream, regardless of his threat, she felt something hard and round poke into her side. It was a weapon. Nothing else could feel like that. If she screamed, she died. If she held on, there was always a chance she could escape.

"Good girl," he said, his lips so close to her ear it made her wince. "I'm going to take your purse now. Don't do anything stupid."

"Fine. Take it. Take the money. There are credit cards. You can take it all."

He didn't respond. Just lifted the purse from her grasp. The gun still poked her side. She couldn't see what he was doing, but she knew that he wouldn't have to look hard for her keys. She kept them in the outside pocket so she herself wouldn't have to dig for them. Stupid. Another bonehead move. She lived in D.C., for God's sake, one of the most dangerous cities in America, and she walked around like she was invincible. Even after she'd sensed someone was stalking her.

He unlocked the car electronically, then pulled her back so he could open the back door. ''Put the packages in the back seat.''

She did as he said.

He opened the front door. ''Get in.''

She did, searching frantically for something to use as a weapon.

He'd already figured this part out, because the second she was behind the wheel, he captured her hands, held her wrists with one hand while he tied them together with a thick blue scarf. Then he tied that to the wheel.

A moment later, he ran around the car. She pulled at her restraint, tried to move so that at the very least she could honk the horn, but then he was beside her. Him and the gun.

''I won't hurt you. Just listen to me. I'm going to untie you. You're going to drive away from here. Don't panic, and don't try anything stupid, and we'll both get out of this alive.'' He stuck her key in the ignition and undid the bindings. ''Start it up. Now.''

With trembling fingers, she turned the key. From her peripheral vision, she saw him toss the Santa hat and the ridiculous beard into the back seat. His hair was dark, his skin, pale. She was afraid to look at him directly, afraid that if he realized she could identify him, he'd have no reason to let her go.

''That way,'' he said, pointing with his free hand toward the east exit.

She checked her mirror, then, without even thinking about it, she turned his way, and something registered. She'd seen him before. Recently.

''Drive.''

She focused on her speed, direction and the gun he held so steadily he couldn't possibly miss. But the face haunted her. Where had she— "You're that reporter. You killed that old man."

He grunted. "Yeah. I'm that reporter."

Max Travis. His name made everything else fall into place. All the reports on the news, in the paper. He was a lunatic, and he'd already murdered once. Twice wouldn't make him blink an eye.

"You can't get away with this," she said, hoping her voice sounded a lot stronger than she felt.

"I already have."

Chapter Two

"Where are we going?" Jade was scared, but kept her fear under control. If she was to escape this ordeal alive, she would have to be ready to flee at the first opportunity.

"Shut up. Turn right here." The gun in Max's hand never wavered. Damn that CSI show—she could picture the bullet entering her body, tracing a path to her heart… Her purse lay at his feet, so she couldn't get to her cell phone or the mace.

"Can't we talk about this?"

"No. Head for I-95."

Jade threaded her way through the streets of Arlington for the highway, fully aware that it headed for either Washington or deeper into Virginia. She considered faking a skid on the snow-swept streets, but the gun could go off in a crash.

"Get on here," Max said, waving the gun toward the southbound on-ramp.

She swung onto the highway, merged with the traffic and accelerated into the blowing snow. She reached to turn the heater up and Max's nervous twitch reminded her that she was being kidnapped by a cold-blooded killer.

She tried to recall what she'd heard about the man on the news—pitifully little, actually—that might help her reason with him. He was a reporter for the *Washington Post.* He'd done some big stories, some undercover work. He'd even been up for a Pulitzer. For unknown reasons, he'd brutally murdered an older man, a friend of his father's and an important man at Geotech, an energy and mining company large enough to change the course of the nation for years. Even the FBI, often loathe to meddle with the D.C. police, was involved in the hunt for this man. His father said the murder was totally uncharacteristic, that Werner Edwards was a family friend. He swore Max would be exonerated.

Oh yeah, she felt much better now. All his neighbors probably thought he was a real nice guy. Never hurt a fly.

"Pull off at the next exit."

"We're going to Springfield?"

"Just pull off."

Jade did as she was told, and Max directed her through turn after turn around the suburban streets.

She watched him as closely as she could as he divided his attention between her and the streets, peering out between the gusts of snow, then back at her. "Stop. Stop here."

Again, she did as she was told, pulling behind a black SUV on a quiet, windblown street.

"Turn the car off."

She did, her hand shaking, her heart in her throat.

Was this the end? Was he going to kill her here? In the middle of suburbia?

From beside him, on top of the Santa suit, Max withdrew the blue scarf. ''Crawl through to the back seat and lay down.''

''No. Please.''

He waved the gun at her, a new sense of urgency and desperation to his moves. She obeyed, the fear making her clumsy. She finally made it to the back seat where he forced her to kneel on the floor. ''Put your hands behind your back.''

''Don't hurt me. My father can help you—''

''Your father's the reason you're here.''

''My father? What does he—''

''Put your damn hands behind your back.''

The seats pressed into her stomach as she worked her arms around until her hands were in the small of her back, and Max tied them tightly. ''Lay down on the seat.''

''I can't.''

Max grunted and opened the door. As the cold swept across her bare legs, Jade realized how exposed she was, but he quickly closed it, then opened the rear door. He tossed the presents into the back with his free hand. Once the seat was cleared, he pulled her roughly onto the cushions and pulled off the thick black belt from his Santa suit. He used it to tie her ankles together.

''One more thing,'' he said and pulled a neckerchief from his pocket.

''No.''

''I can't have you scream.'' He crawled onto the seat with her. He didn't hurt her, in fact, he moved carefully, making sure his knee was on the seat and not her body, but the closeness, his proximity, made her flesh crawl and it was all she could do not to pass out.

He forced the cloth between her teeth and tied it behind her head. "I'm going to be out of the car for a few minutes, but I'll be watching you. Don't be stupid." Max waved the gun in front of Jade's terrified eyes, then slammed the door.

As she lay face down on the back seat, the sound of his footsteps disappeared rapidly in the winter wind. She tested her bonds, but whatever other flaws Max might have, tying knots badly was not among them.

She tried squirming around so she could push herself upright against a door, but the necessary movement caused both her coat and her dress to ride up her thighs, and she felt horribly vulnerable, so she lay quietly and tried to think of a way to escape.

She heard scraping at the back of the car, but couldn't tell what it was.

The mace and her phone were so close, and yet there was no possibility of getting them. No one knew where she was. The moronic detective had stopped tailing her. Her father wouldn't even miss her for a few more hours, and then what? They'd look at the mall, but had anyone seen her abduction? The crowds that had been so pressing inside the stores had vanished in the far reaches of the parking garage, so she couldn't count on any witnesses. Even if they had seen her, she'd been kidnapped by Santa Claus. She doubted they'd even start looking for her car for hours, and with this snow…

Overwhelmed, frightened beyond any kind of reason, she blinked frantically as hot tears blurred her vision. She couldn't move, she couldn't speak, God, at least she wanted to see. But the tears wouldn't stop.

The driver's door opened with another blast of cold wind and gusting snow. She heard his coat rustle, the SUV tip slightly with his weight. Then his voice. "You okay?"

She tried to tell him she was not okay, that she'd never be okay again, but she couldn't with the gag in her mouth.

He turned on the interior light and looked over the seats at her.

All she could do was blink, trying to clear her vision.

"Legs cold?" he asked.

That startled her. What the hell did he care if she were cold? She didn't want to answer, but the fact was, her legs were freezing. She nodded once, then turned her head so she faced the back of the seat.

She heard the rustle of cloth, then her coat slipped down to mid-calf. More rustling, then more of her legs were covered. She twisted around so she could glance down, and saw the red of the Santa suit across her ankles.

He started the car, slowly edged into the street. As he drove, she shifted on the seat until, when she craned her neck, she could just see out the top of the side window. She tried to guess where they were from her limited field of vision but it was useless, and she quit trying. She needed to conserve her energy. He had to stop sometime.

She tried to focus on sounds, anything at all familiar, but the big luxury car had been designed to keep traffic noise out. All she could tell was when they got on the highway again, by the speed of the car and the occasional sound of a truck going by.

Time crawled by as he drove and drove, and every minute seemed to reveal a new ache, a new pain, a new terrifying facet of her situation. Her arms cramped in the unnatural position and no matter how she lifted them, shifted them, the pain just worsened. Even her ankles hurt, as the edge of the thick belt chafed.

Her ribs hurt, her head throbbed, and she'd gotten stuffed up from crying and had to struggle for breath beyond the gag in her mouth.

It felt as if she would surely die from the fear, if nothing else. Image after image of what he could do to her flooded her brain, only to be followed by vivid mental pictures of her father hearing the news that she was dead.

A lurch, and her eyes opened.

God, she'd slept. It seemed impossible. But she had slept, for how long, she had no clue.

She realized that the very absence of noise and motion was what had awakened her. The driver's side door opened and her kidnapper got out, then the rear door opened and she once again felt cold air on her legs.

''Just a second and I'll have your legs untied,'' he said. She felt him fumbling with the belt, but was still unable to answer with the gag in her mouth.

With her legs free, he awkwardly helped her out of the back seat. Once she was standing, he undid the gag.

She swallowed several times, moved her aching jaw. She wished her hands were free because she felt so unsteady. ''Where are we?''

''Someplace safe. Come on.'' He took hold of her arm and pulled her along, at first quickly, but after she stumbled, he slowed the pace. He opened a door, and the light temporarily blinded her.

''I don't feel safe,'' she said. She blinked her eyes several times as they adjusted to the light. She took in her surroundings.

They stood in a large one-room cabin. There was a kitchenette to their right, a small table with four chairs around it, a desk against the wall to the left below a small window. On the other side, a half wall blocked her view of what she assumed was the bathroom. Across the room a double bed complete with a brass headboard sat below a second window. The door behind her led to the enclosed garage.

The decor was simple, rustic. Wood dominated everything, including the floor, which only had a few area rugs to lend warmth. There were two pictures on the wall, but they were both landscapes, nothing that would give her a clue as to the personality of the man who'd kidnapped her. It was neat, tidy, but it felt like it was more of a vacation cabin than a real home.

Max quickly shed the remains of his Santa outfit to reveal a pair of gray slacks to go with his light blue dress shirt. He recovered his gun from the kitchen counter and came back to Jade. ''Turn around.''

She did so, facing the wall, and he untied her hands, then pulled off her coat.

''Go sit at the desk.''

‘‘Why? You need some typing or something? I don’t—’’

He poked her with the gun barrel. ‘‘Just do it.’’ She walked to the desk chair, and Max pulled it around so it faced the room. ‘‘Sit. Put your arms on the rests.’’

She did, and using both the blue scarf and the rope he expertly tied her to the chair. He put the gun on the table and moved to the sink. ‘‘Do you want some water?’’

Her mouth was terribly dry. An almost metallic aftertaste reminded her of the gag, the terror of feeling so helpless. Water wouldn’t fix that, but she was thirsty. ‘‘Please.’’

She watched as he got a glass and filled it. He looked harried. With one hand, he grabbed one of the chairs from the small table. He set it down with the back toward her, straddled the seat and tilted the glass to her lips so she could drink.

She gulped awkwardly, spilling a thin stream of liquid down her chin. She had to turn her head when she was through and more water dripped down to her dress. Her cheeks heated with embarrassment despite the illogic. It wasn’t her fault she was tied up like this.

He set the glass on the desk, then walked over to the fireplace on the opposite wall. The wood had already been laid, kindling and all, and it took him only a moment to get a nice blaze going. He stared at the fire as it swelled, then walked back to where she sat. He knelt in front of her. She tried to scoot back until he slipped off one of her shoes, then the other. He stood, his expression somehow scarier because of its neutrality, walked back to the fireplace and put her shoes on the hearth. "They'll warm up soon," he said.

The act unsettled her as much as anything had. This odd, desperate man who'd kidnapped her at gunpoint was concerned about her feet being cold?

He joined her again, sitting on the other chair with his arms folded across the back.

"Look, I hadn't planned this."

"Yeah. Right. You just happened to have rope and scarves in your suit. What do you want? Money? I can get—"

"I don't want your money. I told you that at the mall." Max shifted his gaze to the wall behind her, his face losing all expression. What remained was exhaustion, worry. Fear.

"Then why? What the hell do you want from me? Are you some kind of pervert or something?"

Max laughed weakly. "Well, I'm not this kinky. I just—I'm at the end of my rope." He shifted his gaze back to meet hers, and for the first time she really noticed how blue his eyes were. Despite the fact that they were so bloodshot. His left eye even had a tiny twitch.

"Why did you kill that old man?"

"I didn't kill him. Werner was like an uncle to me." He briefly closed his eyes and the grief shadowing his face surprised her. Or was it guilt?

"Then why not turn yourself in? Look, if I get home safely, I'll just forget all this—unpleasantness. My father has some power in D.C. We could help—"

Max stood, almost knocking his chair over. ''Your father is the reason I'm in this mess.''

He'd mentioned that before. Obviously he was unbalanced and she needed to tread lightly. She made sure her voice was soft, non-threatening. ''What are you talking about?''

Max paced the small room like a tiger in a cage. ''Your father. And Geotech. Christ, I've tried everything. Even my own editor can't wait to see my head on a pike outside the city walls. You have to know the senator is in it up to his eyeballs. I know you two work together, that you're his assistant. So please, do us both a favor and cut the bewildered act.''

If Jade could have faded into the desk chair, she would have. She was stunned by the vehemence in his voice. ''I don't have a clue what you're talking about.''

He stopped in the middle of a frenzied stride and looked at her. His shoulders slumped as he ran both hands through his dark hair.

Staring at her, measuring her, obviously wondering if he should believe her, his lips curved in a wry smile, and he sat on his chair again. ''If you're lying you're damn good at it.''

''I'm not lying.''

That smile again, mellowed with a sadness that was palpable. ''When your father first got on the Ways and Means committee, Geotech was a relatively small company, but with big ambitions. Their basic approach was deals and mergers, lots of investor cash, but few real assets. They approached Senator Parker for political assistance, but he turned them down cold, unsure of their stability, and unwilling to expose himself and the country to the risk.''

Jade remembered that time. Mom had still been alive, and there had been lively discussions about the viability of the company. Her dad had been dubious about their entire approach. ''Okay, so what's that got to do with murder and kidnapping?''

''Flash forward a few years. Geotech found the support they wanted in Texas. Their stock flew out of the brokerages at ever higher prices, and they rapidly became a more-or-less respected organization, one of, if not the, biggest energy brokers in the country.

''Meanwhile, your father became more powerful, wielding the kind of influence that gets bills passed. Then your mother died.''

''My mother?''

His mouth curved in an apologetic smile. ''She's only relevant because your father's grief made him an easy target for Geotech. He started gambling, which Geotech was happy to exploit. They made sure your father would gamble to his heart's content. And now he owes them somewhere in the arena of ten million dollars, peanuts compared to the hundreds of millions the new energy bill is worth to them. Now they're blackmailing him for his vote.''

''That's a lie.'' Jade's hands shook at the thought. ''Dad would never submit to that kind of blackmail. Which is irrelevant because he doesn't gamble and would never have incurred that kind of debt.''

Max smiled at her, his gaze assessing her carefully. ''A man will do almost anything to protect his name and reputation.''

She shuddered, his message not lost on her. ''You

are crazy. I'm Dad's executive assistant. There's no way he'd be that deep in the hole without me knowing about it."

"Right." Max's smile faded to grimness. "I figure you're either unaware of his problem, or you don't know what to do about it."

"No. You're wrong about this. And what's that got to do with that old man you killed?"

Max leaned forward. "I told you. I didn't kill him. Werner was finally persuaded to be on the board at Geotech, and when he found out what was going on, he talked to my dad and then to me. He knew all about your father's debt, the gambling. And that Geotech wasn't above blackmail. That's why he was killed."

Exhaustion suddenly swept through Jade. Max was obviously one of those people who had seen so many bad things that he'd been overwhelmed, seeing conspiracy everywhere. She doubted he would listen to reason. "I see."

Max met her gaze. "You remember something?"

She saw a flash of reason in his eyes and hope boosted her spirits. "There's probably a bunch of stuff I missed on my dad's computer. You know, if we just went to the Senate Office Building, we could probably…"

"Damn it." Max stood and swept his chair over with one angry wave of his hand.

Jade cringed. Had she pushed him over whatever edge of sanity remained?

"You're good, lady."

"What do you mean?"

Max glared at her, his desperation obvious. ''I'm not stupid, Jade. You will tell me what you know.''

''I don't know anything other than that you're wrong. My father is an honest, hard-working public servant. He would never allow himself to be compromised.''

He snorted. Shaking his head, he walked to the television and turned it on.

''You know, if you untie me, I'll be a lot more likely to listen to reason.''

''Right.'' Max moved to the refrigerator and opened it, the commercial for maxi-pads coming from the TV as incongruous as it was uncomfortable. ''You have a choice between the frozen fried chicken, or the frozen meat loaf dinner.'' He opened the packages and put them in the oven.

''Super.'' Jade shifted uncomfortably. ''Uh—Max? I could use a bathroom visit.''

He looked at her for a moment as if he didn't believe her. But after a sigh, he came to her chair. ''Yeah, okay.'' He untied her and with a hand on her elbow, escorted her to the bathroom.

''Thanks.'' She stepped inside and reached to close the door, but he stopped it with his hand.

''Don't be long.''

''I wanted to wash up a bit.''

His gaze swept the small bathroom, lingering on the useless miniscule window, and then he gave her a curt nod.

She closed the door, sank against it and sighed. Decorated in the same rustic fashion as the rest of the cabin, the bathroom walls were paneled wood. Two pictures hung above the commode, both antique prints of Victorian women on washday. The sink had a rust stain running under the spigot, but it looked clean enough. The floor, a spotted linoleum, had two area rugs, both in a shaggy brown. Sure enough, there was no way out other than the door.

She turned the water on in the sink and used the sound to cover a quick search of the medicine cabinet and drawers, but there was nothing that she could use as a weapon. Only a few personal items: aspirin, a comb, toothpaste, some new toothbrushes, floss. The only razor was electric, and she doubted she could shave him into letting her go.

Hurriedly, she washed her hands and face.

She turned the water off and, through the thin wall, heard Max moving about in the kitchen. If she could get to the car and get her cell phone…

As cautiously as she could, she opened the bathroom door and crouched behind the half wall. The door to the garage was only a few feet away. She hadn't noticed before, but the wood floors were cold. Her toes, encased in nothing but panty hose, curled.

She started when Max called out. "How you doing in there?"

She held her hand over her mouth to muffle the sound and said, "Fine. Out in a minute." With her heart pounding so loudly she was surprised he couldn't hear it, she detected movement near the stove. If he stepped out past the wall, there was nowhere to hide.

She made the mad dash, holding her breath, and reached for the doorknob, turned it. The door opened silently and she edged into the darkness of the garage and held the door until it closed.

The cold concrete was worse than the floor inside and she stumbled forward until she bumped into the car. She wasn't a hundred percent sure, but she thought he'd dropped her purse on the floor on the front passenger side.

With shaking fingers, she felt her way around the car. The hood still held a hint of warmth from their trip, but the rest of the metal was cold.

When she reached the passenger door, she touched the frigid handle and took a deep breath. She planned her actions—open the door, climb in and hit the locks, then grab the purse, dig out the cell phone and dial 911. The Virginia police could triangulate the phone, and she could hold Max off with the mace.

She let her breath out with a whoosh and opened the door.

As it registered that there was nothing at all on the floor of the car, the garage suddenly flooded with light. Max stood in the doorway, her purse in one hand and the gun in the other, pointed right at her head.

His eyes were more sad than angry, and so was his voice, when he said, ''Are you looking for this?''

Chapter Three

Dinner was a glum affair. Max had hauled a pair of handcuffs from his luggage, and Jade found herself eating her meat loaf dinner with only her right hand, her left shackled to the chair arm. She was aware that Max had stuck his gun under his butt, where he could grab it if she made so much as a move. Despite her attempts to get him talking, he'd been sullen and silent since he'd pulled her in from the garage.

Max, looking even more haggard, gnawed at the fried chicken. He avoided her glances. The television droned in the background.

She ate, even though the meal tasted like cardboard. She hadn't had a TV dinner in years, but they couldn't actually taste this awful. Fear tainted everything, including her taste buds.

As she forced another spoonful of mashed potatoes in her mouth, Jade noticed there was a third fork partially hidden by a stack of paper napkins. It wasn't much, but it was something. If she could get it. She pushed her cup forward. ''Could I have more coffee?''

Max grabbed her cup and went behind the counter to fill it. "That's one Sweet 'n Low?"

"Please." She was surprised he'd remembered, but it didn't slow her down as she grabbed the extra fork and slid it uncomfortably in her bra. She had to push it to the side so it wouldn't be noticeable, and it poked her just under the armpit.

Max set the cup near her and resumed his seat, eating silently and staring at the table.

"You can't blame me for trying to escape."

Max looked at her, bleary-eyed. "No, I can't.

"I could get you money, legal help."

Max laughed wryly. "How long have you been in D.C., Jade?"

"My whole life, basically."

"And you've been around politics all that time, right? Directly involved for what, ten years or so?"

"What's your point?"

"I've kidnapped a senator's daughter. The odds of my getting a break legally lie between zero and none. Even presuming you're not lying, the best I could hope for would be not getting shot as I turned myself in. Not to mention that if the Geotech people think you're working with me now, I've endangered your life, too." He stared at his plate for a long moment, then looked back at her. "If you are innocent in all this I'm sorry for that part."

"Aren't you being a little melodramatic?"

"C'mon, Jade. Money and power is what drives the government. Why would a man making millions run for president to make a couple hundred thousand a year? Power. Your father's also a powerful man, and there are hundreds of millions riding on his vote.

Hell, wars have been started just so people could make money. What's a few deaths to these people?''

Jade shook her head vehemently. ''You don't know my dad.''

''I wouldn't count on that. At the very least, I know another side of him.'' Max put his fork down and pushed away his half-finished meal. ''Tell you what. I'll give you the benefit of the doubt. Tomorrow I'll show you what evidence I have. It's enough to at least make you listen.''

''Why tomorrow? Show me now.'' Of course she still didn't believe he had anything that would indict her father, but if she could keep him talking, gain his trust…

''No, we both need to get some rest.''

Jade craned her neck uncomfortably to look over her shoulder at the single bed, the fork digging into her side. ''Uh, about that. I'm assuming there isn't a guest house? A separate bedroom in the attic?''

''We're stuck together.'' Max looked at the double bed, then back to Jade. ''I told you before. This wasn't planned. I wanted to talk to you.''

She jiggled her shackled wrist. ''So you just happen to have handcuffs in case of random kidnapping emergencies?''

He met her gaze again. ''I got them in a sex shop when I did a story a few years ago. It was about suburban kink.''

''Oh boy. I feel much better now.''

''Don't worry. I'm way too tired to bother you even if I wanted to. Hell, I've been following you for two weeks.''

''I had the feeling someone was stalking me.''

"Stalking." He winced. "I wouldn't put it that way."

"I have news for you, Max. Kidnapping sounds a lot worse."

"Kidnapping. Murder." He laughed, a hollow sound. "You're my only hope. How's that for ironic?"

"I see your point, but I swear, I can't help you."

"No?"

She sighed with disgust. Delusional but earnest, she'd give him that. But his conviction made him dangerous and she had to remember that, too. "How did you avoid the detective?"

"Some of it was luck. But I've been an investigative reporter for a long time. Generally I know what I'm doing. Although for the past few weeks, I've felt as if I'm in a David Cronenberg film. Very Kafkaesque, if you know what I mean."

"Yeah, I'm a little out of my reality zone, myself. I should be home, wrapping presents. Sipping a cup of sugar-free cocoa."

He looked over at her TV dinner, shook his head. Opened his mouth, but didn't say anything. Instead, he got up, tossed his dinner in the trash bag under the sink and then unlocked the handcuffs.

When she stood, he moved the chair in front of the television and then re-cuffed her. Then he pulled the desk chair next to her so that her cuffed hand was closest to him. He looked tired, exhausted. As if he wouldn't make it through the opening headlines. "Pay attention," he said yawning. "Maybe you'll catch your fifteen minutes of fame."

Her interest piqued. God, she hoped it had been

reported that she was missing. ''Just for my own edification, how long do you plan to hold me prisoner?'' she asked, her attention fully on the tube.

''As long as it takes me to prove Geotech paid off your father and give the cops another direction.''

''Besides you.''

''Wait.'' Max raised his hand as his image appeared on the screen.

''...new development in the Werner Edwards murder that shocked the capital.''

His picture flashed on the screen. He looked like a normal guy, a nice-looking man, in fact. Not in the least crazy.

''Nice pic,'' Jade said.

''Hush.''

''Travis is accused of breaking into *Washington Post* security files. Coworkers still maintain his innocence, although his editor admitted that his fleeing did look suspicious. In other news...''

Max got up and turned the television off. ''Damn it. I've got to call Herb.''

''Leave it on.''

He frowned. ''Obviously they don't know I've grabbed you, or they would have reported it. They've accused me of everything else.''

''Yeah, but don't you want to know if they've discovered I'm missing?'' He flipped the television back on, but there was no mention of Jade. When the broadcast turned to sports, he shut it off.

Jade sighed. She'd been tired when she'd left the office—God, was it only a few hours ago? Now she was exhausted. She was painfully aware of the fork secreted in her bra and felt she had only enough energy for one more escape attempt.

Max stood mutely for a few seconds, then turned to his open suitcase. He pulled out a set of men's blue flannel pajamas. "Here." He dumped thc top in her lap.

She looked at the lanky, muscular man standing tiredly before her, then at the flannel pajama top. "What about the bottoms?"

"This is all I have." One side of his mouth lifted. "Unless you want me to sleep naked."

Damned if she'd take the bait. She rattled the handcuffs. "I'm not sure this is gonna work."

He hesitated, his mouth settling in a grim line before he undid the cuffs and hung them on the arm of the desk chair.

Jade rubbed her wrist, picked up the pajama top and headed slowly for the bathroom with Max close behind her. She stood in the doorway and looked at him. "Can I take a shower?"

He gave her a long hard look. "Pull another stunt like you did earlier and you stay cuffed, period."

Holding her tongue, she closed the door. As soon as she stood alone in the tiny bathroom, she pulled the fork from her bra and set it on the sink. She took a deep breath and tried to relax.

Okay, she'd have to at least run the shower, or he'd get suspicious. What the hell, it might wake her up. She looked around for a hanger, but of course there wasn't one.

There was, however, a hook on the back of the door, and Jade stripped off her clothes and hung them up. There were two bath towels on the rack, and she wrapped one around herself then quickly brushed her teeth, as aware that her kidnapper was standing only a few feet away as if there were a window in the door. She stepped to the shower and adjusted the water.

MAX LEANED AGAINST the wall opposite the bathroom door. He closed his eyes, listening to her move behind the thin walls and thinner door of the bathroom. Oddly, he got a little excited imagining how she looked as she hung her clothes on the back of the door. When the water began in the shower, his thoughts took an even more vivid turn. He pictured her bending over, turning the faucets…

He shook off the thought, angry at himself and his idiot libido. To say now was not the time was a major understatement. Five minutes, ten, and he could finally sleep. Christ, maybe it had been a mistake, grabbing her. He should have just let Peter keep digging.

Too late for should haves. He'd run out of options. She was his only hope, and, assuming she wasn't up to her eyeballs in it, she had to believe him. He wished he had more.

None of it mattered to Werner. Or his wife. His grandchildren. They'd lost him, all because Werner had tried to do the right thing. Max was sure the man had had evidence. He wouldn't have approached Max on a hunch alone.

But now his own course was set. Tomorrow, if not tonight, the powers-that-be would realize Jade was missing and that his car had been abandoned in the mall parking lot.

And he thought things were bad now.

Max laughed without humor. He wished he could

call his father and reassure him, but even if the police hadn't tapped that phone yet, Geotech probably had.

The sound of the shower lulled him, and he let his eyes close again, imagining the steam rising from Jade's shoulders, her wet hair streaming darkly across her breasts….

His eyes clicked open and he realized the shower was no longer running. He'd fallen asleep standing up and had no idea how long he'd been out of it. At least the bathroom door was still closed.

He heard her move around, probably drying herself, then slipping into the pajama top. He should give her the bottoms, too. Hell, he didn't need the distraction of her long bare legs.

The door opened, and he had a view of green eyes surrounded by dark ringlets of damp hair, surprisingly tanned flesh and the soft curve of breasts peeking from the V-neck of his pajamas. He blinked at the vision as she drove forward with all her strength, slamming him against the wall and stabbing at his face with a fork.

Max's left hand came up reflexively and the four tines dug into his forearm. He swung his right fist upward, caught himself at the last second and grabbed her wrist, then twisted until she let go of her makeshift weapon with a sharp animal cry.

Ignoring his pain, he grabbed her around the waist and threw her over his shoulder, then carried her across the room as he felt her stretch to reach the gun at his waist. He threw her on the bed, then turned and smoothly plucked the handcuffs from the chair arm and turned back to her.

Jade scrambled to regain her feet, but he pushed

her back onto the bed and straddled her, fighting for control of her left arm. She tried to hit him again, but he managed to secure one cuff on her wrist and quickly snapped the other end to the brass headboard, then stood, panting, as she struggled for a second and then gave up in despair.

"Please," she said, gasping for air.

His eyes dark with fury, his breathing ragged, he said, "I wish you hadn't done that."

MAX CAME OUT of the bathroom bare-chested, a strip of fabric tied clumsily around his arm, the gun in his other hand. The pajama bottoms rode low on his hips, and his stomach was flat and well defined.

Although he still had a five-o-clock shadow, she could see that his chin was a strong support for the rest of his face and that even haggard, he was a good-looking guy.

He eyed her intently, then walked to the other side of the room to the table. After a moment's hesitation he put the gun down. Running a hand through his dark wet locks, he approached her as she lay on her side on the bed. Anger lingered in his gaze as it locked with hers.

"Sit up."

"Why? What are you going to do?"

His look made her struggle to a sitting position, her heart pounding, her breath trapped in her throat. She knew she'd really pissed him off. "What are you going to do?"

"Frisk you."

She swallowed, trying to clear the way for air. "I don't have anything else. No weapons. No forks."

"For your sake, I hope not."

"This is hardly necessary." She mumbled as he placed his hands on her shoulders, then eased them down to her ribcage. She held her breath as his fingers grazed the outside curves of her breasts.

Her face heated as he continued his search, touching her sides, her back, the curve of her behind.

"Okay," he said, stepping back and yanking down the covers. "Go ahead and lie down."

"But I—"

"That wasn't a request." His mouth set in a grim line, he hardly looked receptive to argument.

She did as he asked and, to her surprise, he tucked the covers around her shoulders. She stayed quiet and watched him move about the small area, turning off lights, then saw him approach as a darker shadow in the night. He crawled across her, touching her as little as possible, and snuggled in under the covers himself.

She shrunk away from him but he didn't seem to notice. In seconds his breathing slowed into the steady rhythm of sleep.

Sleep refused to come so easily to her. She closed her eyes and tried to relax, replaying the day in her mind, wondering if she couldn't have done something, anything to have stopped this before it had started.

She wondered if her father was still awake. He'd undoubtedly missed her when she hadn't returned to the house. Had he called the police? The FBI? Had he told them she'd been stalked?

She peered over at the man beside her. What if Max Travis wasn't the madman he appeared to be?

Despite her escape attempts, he hadn't molested her or really harmed her in any way.

Once they were in the cabin, she hadn't felt terribly threatened. Which didn't make a whole lot of sense. She'd read about Stockholm Syndrome, where kidnap victims came to display a strange association with their captors, identifying with them while fearing those who sought to end their captivity. Only, that tended to happen after a much longer period of captivity.

The thing was, she knew Max had his facts all screwed up, but if he truly believed what he was telling her, then his actions made a kind of twisted sense. Of course her father wasn't involved in any gambling and he certainly wasn't being blackmailed. The only reason she could possibly come up with to lend credence to Max's accusations was the fact that her father had shifted his opinion on Geotech. With his change of heart, the rest of the committee was certain to give the massive energy contract to the company.

Although she'd been surprised by his actions, it wasn't unprecedented. As her dad had explained, he'd done more research and when he'd learned more about the company, he'd decided to change his position. It was one of the great things about him, his willingness to learn, to change, to admit publicly that he had made too quick a judgment. But to someone on the outside, who didn't understand his integrity, it could look suspicious.

Tomorrow, Max was going to show her his evidence. She'd use the opportunity to enlighten him about her father. If she was reasonable, listened respectfully, perhaps Max would come around. She still wasn't sure he hadn't killed his father's friend, so she'd have to watch her step, but he hadn't acted like a psycho or anything. Delusional, yes. Dangerous? The jury was still out, but her instincts said no.

Then again, Ted Bundy had supposedly been a real charming guy.

Ah, hell, she was too exhausted to think. She tried to listen for the sounds of distant traffic, but could hear nothing but a faraway airplane. And Max's breathing.

She snuggled down under the covers, a breath away from him, his heat helping to warm her. Tonight she'd force herself to sleep. Tomorrow there'd be another chance for escape.

Chapter Four

Light. Almost blinding light. And something else—her bladder ached. God, she shouldn't have had that last cup of coffee.

She started to get out of bed and remembered—the abduction, her escape attempts, the handcuffs.

Max.

She rolled as best she could and poked him in the ribs with her free hand. "Max. Wake up."

He snorted and turned his back to her.

She poked him again, hard. "Max. Damn it. Wake up."

He rolled back toward her, shading his eyes from the onslaught of light. "Huh?" He blinked several times as though he, too, were catching up on recent events.

"If you don't get me to the bathroom in a very short time, we're both going to be sorry."

He sat up and rubbed his eyes, and Jade stared at his bare chest, sharply defined pecs, a light mat of curly black chest hair.

"C'mon. Move it."

"Okay, okay." He pushed the covers down and

crawled across her, landing on the throw rug next to the bed. From there he stumbled to the chair where he'd draped yesterday's clothes and fumbled in his pant pocket.

"Would you please hurry?"

He grabbed the gun before he turned back. As he moved toward her, she noticed the bulge in the front of his pajamas. She turned her head. Too much information about a man she didn't want to know. He fumbled with the handcuffs, finally getting them unlocked, and she was off the bed and scurrying to the bathroom before he'd taken the key out of the cuffs.

Max walked into the living room area, his feet cold on the bare wood. He shed his pajamas and pulled on his pants, tucking the gun behind his back, suddenly aware that he, too, needed to use the facilities. "Don't take all day," he called. He couldn't hear her response clearly, but was sure there was a "back off" in it somewhere. He sighed and debated turning on the news.

The toilet flushed, and Max headed for the bathroom door again, only to hear the sound of water running in the sink. "What're you doing?"

"Brushing my teeth."

"Can't you wait a couple of minutes?"

"Morning breath. Hang on."

"Jade, please."

She took pity on him, and a moment later, he'd shut himself behind the door.

He knew she was waiting for him to leave so she could finish with her teeth, but even after taking care of business, he still had a bit of a problem, and he didn't want to go into the living room with the tent in his pants.

He grabbed his toothbrush and anointed it with minty toothpaste. He got it as far as his mouth before he realized he'd left her out there on her own. He dropped the toothbrush and threw open the door.

Jade was right outside, holding up her still-wet toothbrush. She blinked at him and shrank back.

Thank God she hadn't run. Not that she could have gotten far. But he didn't need the aggravation. He had to remember to keep her cuffed when he wasn't with her. He sucked as a kidnapper.

Her bare legs drew his gaze, as did her cherry red, painted toenails. He forced himself to look away. "Stay right here."

He went back inside and finished brushing his teeth, leaving the door open so he could keep an eye on her.

JADE WATCHED HIM at the sink, studying the curve of his backside, the breadth of his shoulders. Nothing personal. It was like looking at a piece of art. The important thing was not to look down at his jeans. His arousal had nothing to do with her, but everything to do with Max being a guy. All she had to do was keep her gaze on his face. So the second he opened the door, her gaze went right there. Just like that.

The tent had folded.

Which just proved that he was a normal guy, and she was clearly a perv. She walked into the bathroom and closed the door behind her, glad that he couldn't see the bright red blush on her cheeks. So okay, she had to admit that under ordinary circumstances, the sight of Max's body would generate considerable interest. He didn't have the overbuilt weight lifter's upper body, but he didn't seem to have an ounce of extra fat either. And just enough chest and stomach hair to be interesting, a light trail heading downward from his abs....

Jade shook her head as she turned on the water. Good God, what did it say about her that she'd been kidnapped, stolen from her life by a man who quite possibly was a cold-blooded killer, and she was thinking about his abs? Maybe a therapist wasn't such a bad idea.

She finished in the bathroom, having chastised herself to the point of boredom, and reentered the living room. When she'd first arrived last night, she'd been far too worried about Max to really examine her surroundings, so she took advantage of the moment to look around.

It appeared to be one of those manufactured log cabins, a single large room divided into sections more by furniture than architecture, with the exception of a countertop between the kitchenette and the rest of the room and the half wall by the bathroom. Nothing that clued her to the sanity—or lack thereof—of Max Travis. Nothing that could be fashioned into a weapon.

She bent over the desk and looked out.

Trees. Snow. Tire tracks disappearing into the distance.

Where the hell was she?

Max walked over to stand next to her. "Beautiful, isn't it?"

"If you like the middle of nowhere."

"My dad used to bring me out here hunting when I was a kid. It's in the shadow of the Blue Ridge Mountains."

"Fabulous. So you've got me in rural hell. What's your plan now?"

Max's piercing blue eyes met her gaze. "I'm going into town to make some calls."

"What about me?"

"Get dressed."

She looked down at the blue pajamas, at her bare legs, forgotten in the face of the winter desolation outside. As she headed to the chair where she'd left her clothes, he stopped her with a hand on her shoulder.

"Want some cornflakes?"

"Sure," she said absently, her excitement mounting. If he took her into town with him, she had a much better chance of getting away.

"They'll be ready when you are."

True to his word, when Jade came out of the bathroom, there was a box of cornflakes, a bowl, a quart of milk, a sugar bowl, and a few packets of Sweet 'n Low on the table.

"Only one bowl."

"Like I said. I have some things to do."

"What about me? I'm going with you, right?"

"You won't be bored. You're going to be reading."

Jade stood with her hands on her hips. "You can't just leave me here."

Smiling, he opened his briefcase. "There's all this, and some stuff on my laptop. I don't know how much you'll be able to get through in a couple of hours…"

''Couple of hours?''

''That's how long I figure it'll take me to make some calls, get some more groceries and pick you up some clothes.''

''Clothes?''

''You need some warm shoes, warm clothes.''

Her shoulders sagged. ''So you're not going to let me go.''

''Not yet.'' He sighed. ''I have a friend—someone who's been helping me track down leads—between him and a guy I know with the FBI I'll see if I can't work out a way to get you back without me getting my head blown off. In the meantime, you'll read.''

After she sat, she poured some cornflakes into the bowl, then looked up at him. ''You're going to leave me here alone?''

''Cuffed to the bed, so don't get too excited.''

''What if something happens to you?''

''You mean if the cops stop me?''

She nodded.

''I'll send them back here to get you.''

''Yeah, right.''

He put a hand on her shoulder. ''Believe what you want but I never intended to hurt you.''

Her eyes fell to the bandaged wound on his forearm. ''Better pick up a first aid kit while you're at it.''

He withdrew his hand. ''Finish up your breakfast. I think it would be best if you skipped the coffee until I get back. I don't have any way of giving you room to maneuver when I'm gone.''

As Jade ate, thinking about being chained up for the next few hours, Max piled a stack of papers on the floor near the bedstead and placed his laptop next to them. ''Write your pants, shirt sizes, shoe size, that kind of stuff, on this piece of paper.'' He set a pen down with the paper. ''Anything else?''

''I don't know. I've never been kidnapped before.'' She finished writing and pushed away from the table.

He guided her into position and handcuffed her to the bedstead.

Trying hard not to panic, she took a deep breath, then let it out slowly, calming herself as much as possible, although the thought of being trapped here to die was right there. She believed that he'd be back as soon as he could, but there was always the possibility of a car accident, of him being shot, of…anything. She settled her back against the pillows he'd placed against the wall.

''Probably as good as it's going to get.''

She rattled the cuffs. ''I'm still worried. Something could happen.''

He sat down, his weight dipping the bed. He stared at her for a long moment, his lips pursed and his brows creased. She supposed he'd had the same thoughts. That something unforeseen could occur. ''Tell you what. I'll tell my friend that someone's here. I'll e-mail him right now. I'll say that if he doesn't hear from me in three hours, he should come to the cabin.''

''Where does he live?''

''He'll be in D.C. And don't worry. He's never let me down.''

She nodded. It was more than she'd hoped for.

He opened his laptop, typed for awhile, then went over to the desk, where he plugged the unit into the wall. She heard the familiar squeal of an online connection. It took a lot longer than she'd figured, but then she had a cable connection at home and at the office, so she never had to wait. Finally, he unplugged the computer and brought it back.

"Do you want the TV on?"

"Is there a remote?"

"No. I just picked up a cheapie so I could watch the news."

"Skip it. This should keep me busy." She waved at the computer and the stack of papers.

"Okay, then." Max stood over her chewing his lower lip. "The files that are pertinent are under Geotech. I've written the password on that sticky note." He nodded at the top of the stack of papers. She saw a string of letters and numbers written in a neat hand.

He headed across the room and picked up a heavy jacket, then got the phone line that was still connected to the jack and put that in his pocket. He paused at the garage door. "A couple of hours then."

"Oh boy."

He opened the door and a blast of cold air swept across the cabin as he stepped out. He pulled the door closed behind him.

Jade heard the garage door open. Her car started up and backed out, then the garage door closed again. She kept listening until she no longer heard the engine, until she was left in silence. At least she'd be able to hear when he came back.

As she had last night, she listened for any noise that might indicate she was near other people, but if anything, the blanket of snow outdoors cloaked even more sound than before. She heard a distant creak and it took her several minutes of concentration to realize it was a large tree swaying in the light breeze.

It was so quiet in the cabin that she could hear her own heart beating. A whoosh in the garage marked the water heater turning on, followed mere seconds later by it going off again. She saw a small flurry of snow fall past the window and heard the pattering of a squirrel's feet on the snow-packed roof.

At least she hoped it was a squirrel. In a brief fugue state she imagined herself attacked by rats as she sat chained to the bed. Max would come back and find a bare skeleton chained to the frame like in a horror movie.

To ward off any more sickening images, she picked up Max's laptop and turned it on, watching it boot up quickly. It was not unlike her own, and she clicked a couple of the unfamiliar icons to see what they might be. With any luck, Max might have one new enough to have a wireless connection.

She looked in the system folder, and it did, indeed. She double-clicked it, then held her breath as the laptop attempted to connect. Finally an error message popped up. No carrier to be found.

Damn.

She turned the unit off to conserve the batteries and leaned over the bed as far as she could, looking around the room for a possible escape route, a way out of the cuffs. Nothing. Exasperated, she tugged at her manacled wrist. Nothing budged.

She sighed and relaxed against the pillow. She looked at the stack of papers Max had left. She poked through the pile, noting everything was dated sequentially. She picked up a handful and began looking at them.

Hmm. Receipts, stapled to regular paper with notes. Phone records. Geotech office memos. Her interest piqued, she began to read.

DESPITE THE E-MAIL Max was still worried about Jade. Leaving her there had been a tough choice, but in the end, it was the only thing he could do. He'd briefly considered not cuffing her, but she'd try to escape and that could only end badly. In her high heels, she wouldn't get far, and far was where she'd have to go for help. The cabin's nearest neighbor was about fifteen miles away.

No, his best bet now was to proceed as carefully as he could with his plan and get back safely. At least he wasn't trying to do the drive to D.C. and back, as he'd been doing for the last couple of weeks.

As he approached the outskirts of Ashwood, he decided he'd do the shopping first, the phone calls after. If Agent Bilick traced the call, Max would be back at the cabin before there could be a response.

He hit the small department store first, picking up a couple of pairs of denims, wool lumberjack shirts, warm socks and hiking shoes for Jade. He found a down jacket in her size, then headed into the women's department for underwear. As he eyed the bras and panties, feeling more out of his depth by the second, an elderly woman approached him.

"Not sure we carry anything in your size," she said.

"Oh." Max reddened. "It's not for me."

"That's a joke, son. You look a bit bewildered."

"Oh. Well, I'm picking up a few things for a lady, and I thought she might like some—delicates—to go with them."

"Do you know her sizes?" The woman, in her fifties, peered at him over thick bifocals.

"Here." Max thrust the paper with Jade's sizes into her gnarled hand.

"Hmm. Well, the panties should be okay, but the shirt size makes picking out a bra a little tough."

Max reached for the paper. "Maybe I should just get the stuff later." He could feel the heat in his face.

The woman pulled the paper out of his reach. "Oh, for heaven's sake. We're talking bras here, not your deepest sins. The shirt size tells us how big around she is. We just need to figure out the cup size."

"Cup size?"

"For the bra."

"I know what it is, I just have no idea."

"Come with me." The older woman grabbed his wrist and led him to a bra display. "I'll make this easy for you." She waved at several bras hanging next to each other. "Which of these would she fit into best?"

Max looked them over. Certainly, the large Italian grandmother size wouldn't work on Jade, and she didn't need the padded unit at the other end. His only real frame of reference was when he'd checked her for weapons.

"This looks about right," he said, pointing.

"B cup," the saleswoman said. "We're making progress now." She led him back to the lingerie he'd been looking at before. "You pick out what you want, and I'll get it for you in the right sizes."

"Thanks. Thanks a lot." Max quickly picked out two bra and panty sets and a bathrobe. At the last minute, while his order was being rung, he got a pair of fluffy slide-in slippers. The floor got awfully cold. In short order, he was out of thc department store and headed for the grocery.

Although he'd been living largely on frozen dinners, Max made a serious effort to shop, picking out fresh vegetables, bread, butter, a box of Sweet 'n Low, eggs, a couple of nice steaks, and the ingredients to some of his specialties. At the very least, he could feed her well while she was his captive.

Captive.

He could still hardly believe that he'd taken her. It was something outside his ken, something he'd never considered. He liked her. In fact, if they'd met somewhere else, some other time, he'd have asked her out. God knows, she probably would have turned him down flat, but he'd have gone for it. Not only was she beautiful, but he could already tell she was sharp. Really sharp. Without that, he didn't care if the woman looked like a supermodel, he couldn't sustain interest. For him, it was all about the dialogue. Yeah, okay, the sex, too, but he liked to talk after that.

He finished loading everything into the car, then headed for the gas station at the edge of town.

After filling the big SUV, appalled at the cost, he stepped into the pay phone, pulled out his phone card and began dialing the long sequence of numbers he'd written down before leaving the cabin. Finally, he reached the FBI in D.C.

"Agent Bilick, please."

"Who's calling?"

"Cho Ming."

"Thank you." Music filled the earpiece as Max waited to be transferred.

"Bilick here. And this better be a dead Chinese woman."

"Hey, Herb, it's—"

The agent hung up.

Max sighed. Obviously, Herb recognized his voice. Even protected from the chill wind by the phone booth, his fingers were turning white in the cold, and he had to concentrate to redial the lengthy code for the phone card and then the FBI number.

"Federal Bureau of Investigation."

"Yes, this is Cho Ming. Agent Bilick and I were speaking and we got cut off."

"I'm sorry, sir. I'll reconnect you."

"Thank you." More bad music.

"This had better be important."

"It is, Herb. You've probably heard about my little problem."

The agent snickered. "Little problem? Hell, you're facing a needle in the arm, pal. I hope you're calling to turn yourself in."

"Look, I know we're not exactly friends—"

"Not friends? You got me in so much hot water, I'm still swimming. And don't tell me you didn't bear any responsibility in Cho Ming's death."

"She came to me, Herb. I told her those things had to go through channels, but she didn't think you guys were doing enough. She knew the dangers of going public better than I did. Besides, you came out the hero in the story, remember?"

"That's not how the agency saw it. 'Not a team player' was the nicest thing anybody said."

"It wasn't your fault. You did the right thing."

"Okay. Okay. What do you want? To turn yourself in, I hope. Make me look good for a change."

"Not exactly what I had in mind. I need some help. And before you ask, no, I didn't kill that man."

"If you didn't do it, why did you run?"

"The people behind this have at least some of the D.C. police in their pocket. And probably some of your guys."

The agent sighed deeply. "So you figured you'd put my feet to the fire again? What did I ever do to you?"

"Come on, Herb, this is serious. You know me well enough to know I'm not a killer. I was drugged the night of the murder. At the Guardian. I can't remember much, but I do remember a gorgeous redhead. I'd bet the farm she works for Geotech."

"Geotech? Jesus."

"Also, the second I got home, the cops came, so there's probably surveillance stuff at my apartment. Maybe you can trace that equipment. That morning a D.C. patrolman rousted me on a bench by the Lincoln Memorial. You should be able to find him. Oh, and I'm with Jade Parker."

There was a long silence. Really long. Finally, "Turn yourself in, Max. Do it now."

"Check that stuff out, Herb. I'll get back to you."

"Wait..."

Max hung up. He was shaking. Although any trace would go back to the phone card number, it wouldn't take the feds long to find the phone booth if they wanted to. He had to get back to the cabin as soon as possible. The police were undoubtedly looking for Jade's SUV.

He did the dialing ritual again, this time to Peter's direct line at the paper.

"Peter Shelby."

"Anything new?"

"Jade Parker's missing. At least that takes the heat off you, as far as lead stories go."

"Well, maybe not."

"What?"

"She's with me. And if I see that in the papers with your byline, I may have to commit a murder."

"Holy crap. What the hell are you doing?"

"Hopefully, she's going to get me those Cayman account numbers."

"Why should she? You don't think she's as deep in this as the senator?"

"I don't think she knows about him, Pete. I'm not sure how much she'll do, either."

"Well, I'm still on it with that crooked lawyer. He thinks he might have a guy at one of the banks who can help. And your dad…"

"No! Keep him the hell away from this. These people have killed once. They wouldn't have any compunction about arranging for him to have an accident. Keep on the lawyer, and if I get anything from Jade, I'll let you know. And do me a favor, check your e-mail. I sent you a couple of things."

"Be careful, buddy. It's getting mighty deep around here."

"Thanks Pete. Later."

Max hung up, blew on his hands to warm them, and trotted to the car.

Nearly forty-five minutes later, he pulled the stolen car in the cabin's garage. He closed the garage door, then entered the cabin carrying an armload of groceries.

As he set them on the counter, he met Jade's gaze.

"Maybe you're not so nuts about Geotech, but I can tell you right now my father's not involved," she said.

"Let's get you out of those cuffs, and then we can talk."

"Aren't you afraid I'll run?"

He stopped. "Keep up the sarcasm and I'll leave you right where you are."

"Sorry," she muttered.

"Listen to me. You couldn't get anywhere that would help you or jeopardize my location, but you could get seriously hurt out there, maybe die." He knelt between piles of paper and fumbled with the key.

Jade thought about what he'd said. From what she could see out the window he was probably right. She wouldn't get far even if she could escape. The thought depressed her. As she waited until he'd freed her wrist, she found herself very aware of the cold smell of outdoors that clung to his coat. She rubbed her wrist.

"I picked up a few more things for you. I'll be right back."

As Max exited, Jade, still in bare feet, padded around the table and peeked in the grocery bags. Although she was impressed that he'd gone to some effort to get good ingredients and even a bottle of wine, the fact that he'd gotten enough food for a week concerned her.

She heard him close the car door and she hurried over to the desk chair.

As he struggled with the knob, she resisted the urge to help. He might really have a case against Geotech, but he had kidnapped her, and he was wanted for murder.

Max entered with an armload of packages and made his way to the center of the room in front of her, where he unceremoniously dumped the whole load. ''Not exactly Christmas,'' he said, ''But I hope this stuff works.''

She pulled the chair over to the bags and boxes. As she opened the slipper box, Max turned on the television and perched on the side of the bed, watching her. His gaze was full of expectation, as if he needed her approval for his purchases. Weird.

She pulled out the denims, the nice wool shirts, warm socks. She opened the shoe box and took out one of the hiking boots.

''Try it on.''

''Looks a little large.'' She held the boot up and eyed it skeptically.

''Put the socks on first.''

She pulled on one of the socks and snugged the boot on, redoing the laces and tying them. She stood, one foot booted and the other bare.

''How does it feel?''

''Pretty good.'' She sat back down and pulled the boot off and reached for one of the lingerie boxes. She opened it and peeled back the tissue paper, exposing three bra-and-panty sets, one black, one peach and one red.

"Hope they fit," Max said, as if he were still talking about the shoes.

"Not exactly winter wear." Jade held up the black half-cup bra and flicked the lace trim with a finger.

"Just wanted you to be comfortable."

"I'll let you know. Let's see what else you got." In short order, she'd opened the other two boxes, one of which contained a terry bathrobe and the other a heavy flannel nightgown. She stood, holding the nightgown to her shoulders. "Ooh, sexy."

Max noisily cleared his throat. "Comfort. Just thinking of comfort."

Jade sat in the chair again, the nightgown across her knees, her left foot still bare, and surveyed the pile of new clothes. She shouldn't have tweaked him with that sexy comment, but she couldn't help herself. "We've really got to talk, Max."

"You've read most of the stuff, right?"

Jade shook her head. "Not about Geotech, Max. What is all this?" Her wave encompassed the pile on the floor.

Max looked genuinely bewildered. "What?"

She shook her head again, exasperated. "How long are you planning to hold me against my will?"

Max met her gaze. "I don't know. I wish I had a different plan, but I don't. I hoped that once you realized what was going on with Geotech and your father that you'd want to help."

"Help? Help what? Help a crazy reporter build a case against my dad? Help a murderer get away? Are you high? I want to go home.'' She stood angrily and stared out the window, arms folded across her chest.

''Look here,'' Max said. He grabbed the laptop, found a file and opened it, then brought it over to her. ''Read this.''

''...Senator Parker agreed with Lieberman and many others, saying 'This kind of legislated contract, without competitive bids, is both un-American and unwise.'''

''So what? And what's this quote from?''

''It's from the *Tribune* on August 17. Now read this one.'' Fumbling with the laptop, Max brought up another file, then showed the screen to her.

''...over the objections of many of his colleagues, Senator Parker tersely stated 'I will do all I can to see this legislation passes. Otherwise, no comment.' Can't the man change his mind?''

''That was on October 20. Now look at this.'' Max laid the laptop down and dug furiously at the pile of paper by the bed. He pulled one out and brought it to her. ''Note the date.''

September twenty-fifth. She looked at Max. That was her birthday but obviously that had nothing to do with anything. ''What's this?''

''It's a printout of interoffice e-mails at Geotech. Read the second one.''

She scanned down to the second e-mail header. ''Retik and target SP on board *Irish Mist*. Success assured.'' She read it again, then handed the paper back to Max. ''And all this means...?''

''Someone named Retik took Senator Parker on something, a yacht maybe, called *Irish Mist* and somehow coerced him into changing his vote.''

"Oh, Max. You really are delusional. SP could be anyone. I need some more coffee." She went to the pot while Max put the paper back in its proper sequence.

"But you read this other stuff."

"Look. I agree Geotech seems to have engaged in a lot of both legal and illegal lobbying. Hell, they've spread more money around than Halliburton. But murder? Extortion? That's a mighty big stretch."

Max sat glumly, hands folded, staring at the television.

"There's more. I want you to read it all. Everything."

She sighed. "You're grasping at straws."

"Just read it."

"First I'm going to change." She gathered some clothes from the floor, then looked up at him. "Where's my purse? I need my brush."

He stood and reached in his pocket for her car keys. "In the trunk." He started to throw her the keys, thought better of it and headed for the garage, Jade close on his heels. Once there, he opened the trunk and she retrieved her bag.

She went directly to the bathroom, and the first thing she did was try the cell phone, but the battery was dead. Nope. Not dead. Removed. So Max might be nuts, but he was careful.

What troubled her was his absolute conviction that her father was involved.

She put the phone down on the counter, her hands shaky. She couldn't stop thinking about the e-mail. The one about the *Irish Mist.* She'd heard her father mention the *Irish Mist,* but for the life of her she couldn't remember in what context.

What bothered her was that according to the e-mail, her father would have been on board on her birthday. She distinctly remembered, because he always spent her birthdays with her, but on her last, he'd had something he said he just couldn't get out of. Work. At the office. She was positive that's what he'd told her, and when she'd called him and he hadn't answered, she'd been hurt and confused. She'd continued to try his office until she'd finally had it and gone to bed.

Which didn't mean he was involved in something illegal. Although thinking about it, she realized she'd never questioned him about his whereabouts. Why not?

No, it didn't mean a thing.

She brushed her hair back and put it in a ponytail, then took her time putting on some makeup.

As she exited the bathroom, she saw that Max was by the television, sitting on the wooden chair. He didn't even turn when she walked across the room to the refrigerator. There was orange juice and she poured herself a glass. "Max? Do you want some?"

He didn't respond. In fact, he never turned away from the television. She looked at the show, but it was just the local news, and the story wasn't about her or Max.

He turned to her, a wild gleam in his eyes that made her shiver. "Get your coat. We have to go."

Chapter Five

"What?" Jade's heart pounded with excitement. This could be her chance to get away.

"I said, get your coat." He had already retrieved his from the wall peg.

She didn't argue but quickly put on her coat, then got her purse before he changed his mind. Then she slipped into the bathroom to retrieve her phone. The adrenaline still pumped in her veins.

At the door, he handed her a blue baseball cap. "Put this on."

"Max, what's going on?"

Ignoring her, he entered the garage and waited for her to get into the car.

Jade sat silently as Max skidded her heavy car around and drove slightly too fast down the tracks in the snow, the rear end sluing. For nearly ten minutes they drove through groves and openings before she saw a paved road. "You weren't lying about being in the boonies."

Max smiled grimly and briefly glanced her way before returning his attention to the road, his jaw firmly set, anger and fear radiating from his body.

Something was different about him. Something that made the hair on the back of her neck stand up. God, what had set him off? But she didn't dare push him now.

They bounced across a pile left by a snowplow and he slowed before turning the wheel and guiding the big car along the two-lane road.

"I know you think my father's involved in this," she said, knowing full well this was a horrible time to incur Max's wrath, but she wasn't sure what he was going to do. Maybe she could get the other Max back. The rational man. "For a politician, he's a pretty decent guy. He tries to do the right thing."

"You were adopted."

She started at the non sequitur, but Max's voice had leveled some, and she exhaled a breath she hadn't realized she'd been holding. She looked out at the snowy countryside and shivered, not from the cold. Better to just go along with him. Talk calmly. "I was eight, before my parents adopted me. I've been with them a long time."

He threw her another glance. "Eight?"

She nodded. "I was lucky. That's getting to the age when nobody wants you. It was tough at the orphanage. You'd see all the really little kids getting adopted right away."

"I can see why you'd feel loyal to him."

"Why do you have to twist everything around? I'm loyal because I love him and I don't believe anything you've said about him." She turned to stare at the dismal scenery. "I was intimidated at first. You've seen him, he's a big gruff bear of a man. But Mom was his soft side. They were two sides of the same coin. A real partnership. That's probably one reason I've never gotten married. I've never had anything like that."

"It must have been rough when your mother died."

"It was." She didn't want to continue the conversation, but she could literally feel the difference in Max. He'd calmed considerably, and that made her relax. Not totally, that would be stupid, but at least she wasn't shaking in her boots. When she'd taken the self defense course, they'd told her to try and humanize herself, to create some kind of a bond with an abductor. It was against her nature to go into personal details, especially with a stranger, but this wasn't an ordinary relationship.

"We both depended on her for so much. My father counted on her to maintain his social life, his personal world. She was so good for him. She made sure he left politics outside. She loved to cook." Jade smiled at the flashes of memory that skittered past her mind's eye. "But she was terrible. I mean it, she could ruin spaghetti, which now that I cook, I find amazing. She tried so hard.

"My father never said a word, complimented her to anyone he could. But he always insisted my mother have every social gathering catered, said he needed her to be by his side, not in the kitchen. It wasn't until I was in high school that I figured out his ploy. I think Mom did, too, but she never let on."

Max grunted, nothing more.

She faced his profile, studying his face. It confused the hell out of her, how she could have any kind feelings toward this man. He'd kidnapped her at gunpoint. And yet, she didn't despise him. Feared him, yes. But there was something about him that drew her in. That made her want to understand what was going on inside his head. Maybe it was the contradictions. Apologizing while he tied her up. Buying her the underwear. It was crazy.

Him being a murderer didn't fit. Yeah, yeah, he had all his so-called evidence, but she wasn't talking about that. Her intuition said he wasn't a killer.

As they hit the outskirts of town, Max turned into a service station and pulled over next to the pay phones. He dug in his pockets for change. "I'll be right back."

He slammed the door and the quiet closed in. She wrapped her arms around her waist, prepared to get real cold real fast. Of course he hadn't left the keys.

Her door opened, scaring her into a gasp. She looked up into Max's troubled eyes.

"Come on."

It took her a minute to make her fumbling fingers work to let her out of her seat belt. Heart beating against her chest, she climbed out onto a good two inches of snow. They crunched their way to the phone booth, where he waited for her to enter first. He came in after, squeezing next to her, his clean fresh scent filling her senses, and then closed the door. He dropped some change in and called information, asking for the police station mentioned in the TV report. Once he had the number, he quickly dialed.

A police station? Was he going to turn himself in? Tell them to come get her? She waited, watching as their breath made small clouds of condensation.

Max had no idea why he'd brought Jade with him.

She didn't need to know that he'd screwed up like this. But he also didn't want her sitting alone in the car. She could call out to someone, attract attention. For all he knew, she could hotwire the car.

He inhaled her sweet feminine scent, wondering if it wouldn't have been safer to leave her in the car. Hard to believe she could distract him, with her long legs and expressive eyes. It might be because of her that he was running for his life. That poor Werner had been murdered. Max didn't want to believe she had anything to do with Geotech, but he still couldn't rule out the possibility.

When he finally got connected, he asked for the desk sergeant.

"Sergeant Spector."

He cleared his throat, not sure he wasn't making things infinitely worse for himself. "My name's Max Travis, and I saw on the news this morning that you arrested a man with Jade Parker's license plates."

"Travis?"

"Yes. The Travis who's wanted for murder. I kidnapped Jade Parker, and switched the plates on that guy's car. He's innocent. I chose his car because it was the same model."

"Uh, can you hang on a minute?"

Max laughed. "I don't think so. But you've got a man who knows nothing. The wrong man." Max hung up the phone and looked at Jade. "One more."

Her eyes widened. She looked confused. Good. Maybe she'd start getting a clue. But he couldn't think about her right now. He pulled out the calling card and dialed a long sequence of numbers, then waited for the ads and the ring tone.

''Peter Shelby.''

''Pete, it's me.''

''I don't have anything yet, Max. Geez, give me a—''

''It doesn't matter,'' he said, interrupting. Afraid to stay on the phone. ''I need to use your car.''

There was a long pause. Max knew he shouldn't involve Pete further, but his choices were damned narrow. He wouldn't be upset when Pete said no. Desperate, but not upset.

''Okay,'' he said, drawing out the word. ''Any idea how long you'll need it?''

Max's breath came out in a cold cloud. ''A couple of days. No more. This one's gotten too hot. Can you meet me at Theodore's in Arlington in two hours?''

Pete's sigh drifted over the phone line. ''Yeah, sure. What the hell. What's a little aiding and abetting between pals?''

''I'll make it up to you.''

''You bet your ass you will.'' The line went dead.

''Let's hit it,'' Max said, and Jade pushed the door open. They headed for the car, climbed in, and he swung out on the road headed for the highway north.

He hoped to God Pete wasn't being tailed. No surprise if he was. Max would have to be extraordinarily careful before he tried to make the meet. Or it would all be over.

THE WATERGATE IS one of Washington's most prestigious business addresses. Nestled into beautifully landscaped grounds, its most appealing feature is the view of the Potomac River. Forever destined to be associated with the infamous Watergate hotel, this building resides at the high end of Washington office addresses with 24-hour security, on-site concierge service and a retail arcade that features a U.S. Post Office, grocery stores, a pharmacy, several restaurants, a deli with outdoor seating, banking and ATM facilities and more.

In an office whose studied emptiness only emphasized the resources funding the original Pollack oil painting hanging on the wall and the Ming vase on a Sixth Dynasty teak table, C. J. Harris, wearing a handmade Italian silk suit, sat looking out at the great river. The indirect lighting was so masterfully done that none of the various high-tech devices readily available to him were obvious behind the rosewood and ebony paneling that secured the walls like a huge Chinese puzzle box.

He sat behind a massive teak desk whose shine nearly matched that of his wing-tipped shoes. A sleek Swedish-designed telephone shared the desk with a keyboard and a nineteen-inch flat-screen monitor, but the sheer size of the desk made it appear all but empty.

A small chime sounded, followed by a muted feminine voice. "Mr. Retik is here."

"Send him in." He never ceased his contemplation of the river below. He sat without moving for roughly a minute as the door opened, then shut again with a whisper. Finally, he said, "I'm giving you another chance, Retik."

"How's that, Mr. Harris?"

Harris swiveled his chair about, turned his back to the window and shifted his focus to the figure standing a few feet beyond the desk. "I'm giving you another shot at him. Except this time you're to succeed.''

Although Retik outweighed him by a good seventy-five pounds, none of it fat, his manner was obsequious. ''He should have passed out at the club, Mr. Harris. Your secretary put enough GHB in his drink to down an elephant.'' His cold blue eyes held steady, not a waver. ''The feds are on him now. How long can he stay loose?''

Harris sighed as though dealing with a child. ''That's not the point. The point is that our contract is in jeopardy because you didn't do your job. If the feds get to Travis first, what's to stop him from showing them whatever information he has? Information that could damage our position quite severely.''

''I'm monitoring both the police and the FBI. If he pokes his head up, I'll be there.''

''And that's why it took you over an hour to get here when I sent for you?''

Retik smiled nervously, exposing the silver crown in his lower jaw. ''Yes sir.''

''I see.'' Harris sat with his hands folded and watched Retik squirm. ''And if I told you he'd be poking his head up in Arlington in about—'' Harris glanced at the sleek circle of titanium on his wrist ''—forty-five minutes, I can assume you will take care of it?''

Retik's eyes widened in alarm, then narrowed to a raptor's gaze. ''Yes sir.''

Harris slid a business card across the smooth expanse of desk. ''Please, Retik. No more mistakes.''

The larger man picked the card up and held it in a

burly hand as he looked at the words written on the back. "I'll take care of it." He started for the door.

"Oh, Retik." Harris waited until the other man had turned. "Dispose of the woman, too."

Retik's thin-lipped smile spoke volumes. He nodded and strode from the office.

By the time the door closed, Harris had already resumed his contemplation of the Potomac.

JADE STARED AT the snow-dappled trees and the gently rolling hills as Max drove toward Arlington. She should have paid more attention to the road signs. Instead, she thought about Max. Her thoughts ran faster than the wheels beneath her as she tried to figure out this strange man.

It made a weird kind of sense that he'd called the police. If he was an innocent man on the run then he'd have a particular empathy for someone else being falsely accused. On the other hand, by calling the police, by admitting he'd kidnapped her, he'd done nothing to make his situation better.

She turned to him, watching as his jaw flexed. She could see the tension in his face, the way his hand gripped the steering wheel.

She'd considered the possibility that he planned to let her go in Arlington, but had discarded the notion. He'd dug himself into a pit and she could see no way out. He needed her. Needed her to believe something she couldn't. Not that he was innocent of murder, that wasn't a stretch any longer. But she couldn't put her father in the middle of this morass. Which could mean someone out there wanted Max to believe her father had gotten involved, although it seemed unlikely.

She knew things like this went on. Politics was the biggest game in town, filled with sharks who liked the deep waters of Washington. People did insane, dangerous things to get what they wanted, and the more money that was involved, the more vicious the sharks.

If it hadn't been for the good that power sometimes brings, she'd have gotten out of the game. Yes, she was still that much of a Pollyanna. More people than she cared to think about had told her she wasn't cut out for the life she'd chosen, but she'd made a small difference. In the end, that's all she could hope for. To make a difference. As her father had made a difference.

"About what you did back there," she said finally. "I admire that."

"Nothing to admire. The guy's innocent. I couldn't let him take the fall."

She smiled. "Okay, I'll give you that Geotech could be up to something underhanded, quite possibly illegal. But there's nothing you can say that's going to convince me that my father would have anything to do with it. Especially killing a man over a business deal."

Max sighed as he turned onto the freeway. After he'd gotten into the fast lane, he looked at her, but not for long. His gaze moved back to the road. "For a woman who's grown up in D.C. you're awfully naive, you know that? Do you know how much money we're talking about?"

"I'm not naive. He's my father. I know him. You don't."

"And I'm sure you love him, and think he's the

greatest thing since sliced bread. Even I know he's done some really good things for the country. But he's in over his head. Maybe he's not even aware of what he's doing. I haven't eliminated the idea that he's being coerced. All I'm sure about is that he's involved.''

''It doesn't make any sense. I mean, even the logistics don't add up. Everything goes through me. I write his checks, balance his accounts. I do his personal correspondence. I live in the same house. If he were doing what you said, I'd have noticed something.''

Max looked at her with an unwavering stare. His head pivoted back to face forward, but the effect lingered.

She wasn't being entirely honest. Things had been…off. She wasn't about to leap to the outrageous conclusion that her father was involved in murder, but ever since her mother had died, he'd been different.

It made perfect sense, of course. To lose a life-mate like that would turn anyone's life upside down. It was amazing he was still so capable of handling the heavy weight of his office. And yet, there were absences that had never been adequately explained. He'd developed a nervousness that had worried his doctors. He'd been drinking more than ever before.

All of which could be explained by her mother's death. ''I simply don't buy it. I know him better than anyone. He's a decent man, Max. Yeah, he's made mistakes, but this is way outside the box.''

Max wheeled the big Lincoln through the streets of Arlington and met her eyes as they sat at a stoplight. Niggling thoughts bothered her, little things she'd dismissed. Nothing big, nothing frightening, just off kilter. Why hadn't she questioned her father? Because she trusted him? Or because she hadn't wanted to know the answers?

"Look, Jade." Max said, startling her. "At least meet Peter, talk to him. See if anything he's got to say makes sense."

"But he's helping you. He's prejudiced."

"You're not?"

Max pulled into the restaurant lot and looked for a parking space.

"I know my own father." She folded her arms and looked out her window.

Max braked, hard, jarring her. "Fine." He put the car in park, turned off the engine and handed her the keys. "Sorry for the trouble. I'd appreciate it if you didn't give the police any information about my whereabouts."

Stunned, she cocked her baseball cap and peered at him from beneath the brim. "You're letting me go."

"Yep."

"Why?"

He laughed. "You're really something, know that?"

"I mean, I don't get it. I—" She grabbed the keys before he changed his mind. "I'll talk to Peter."

He didn't say anything for a long moment, then he nodded, opened his door and slid on a pair of dark glasses.

She shook her head. He was right. She was naive. Crazier than he was, apparently. Why didn't she take her car and drive as fast as she could away from him?

It was the call he'd made to the police that had suckered her in. If someone had framed her father or coerced him in any way, then they could have set up Max, too. It wouldn't hurt to at least listen to this Peter. At least she had the keys.

They walked into the coffee shop, and Max scanned the tables for his friend. Although he strode as though he were without worries, his heart pounded. If one person who wasn't Peter recognized him, or Jade for that matter, his flight would be at an end.

Finally, he spotted Peter sitting in the farthest corner. Good man. They'd been through a lot together, but nothing like this. Peter was putting himself in a hell of a lot of danger, helping him like this. They crossed the brown speckled carpet until they reached the booth, then he let Jade slide in first.

"Jeez," Peter said, eyeing Jade with amazement. "Hide in plain sight, huh?"

"Big lunch crowd like this, skulking around would just attract attention." Max waved a hand at Jade. "This is Jade Parker. Jade, Peter."

"You're not gagged and handcuffed. Good sign." Peter smiled, held out his hand across the table. "You're a lot prettier than your pictures."

Jade touched the brim of the baseball cap, glanced down at her over-sized clothes. "After my last twenty-four hours, that's the least of my worries."

"Anyone hangs out with Max here for more than a few hours is in trouble, so consider yourself in good company. I'm just glad you're on the team."

Jade leaned forward, placing her elbows on the table. "I'm not on any team, Peter, except my own. I don't know what Max might have told you, but if you aren't able to convince me in about five minutes that there's some reason for me to stay, I'm gone.''

Peter's gaze shifted to Max. ''Okay, no pressure.'' He took a deep breath, then concentrated on Jade. ''I assume Max filled you in on Geotech. Werner was bringing him a disk with the senator's account numbers in the Caymans—''

''My father doesn't have an account in the Caymans.''

Peter took a sip of coffee. Max knew him well enough to know that he was stalling, getting his arguments lined up. Peter was nothing if not anal retentive. ''Werner thought otherwise. According to my research, this was not a man who exaggerated. Most of the people he'd worked with made a point of mentioning his thoroughness. Said he dotted every I, crossed every T. He had no reason to make this up.''

Jade shrugged. ''I'm not questioning what the man believed to be true. I'm saying he was wrong. Or maybe he was politically motivated to smear my—''

''Not Werner,'' Max said firmly.

She glared at him. ''But it's okay for you to accuse my father of—''

''Uh, could we keep our voices down?'' Peter said, glancing around, and then meeting Jade's eyes. ''I've got a guy working on locating the account numbers. Sorry, but there's a lot of indirect evidence that the senator is involved. That his gambling got way out of control.''

''Indirect evidence? What the hell is that?'' Jade closed her eyes for a moment, then leaned into the table. ''Look. When mom died, dad may have gone a little overboard with the gambling, but nobody got hurt, and it was his money. He got over it. If I'm expected to just sit here and listen to this crap…''

Peter shook his head, then dug in his pocket. He tossed a set of car keys on the table. ''I'm sorry, Ms. Parker. It sucks to hear something like this about someone you care about. For what it's worth, I know what addictions can do. My brother died from a heroin overdose, and believe me, I didn't want to hear it. Maybe if I'd listened I could have helped.'' He looked at Max. ''I'm gonna book. This is too dangerous even for me.''

He stood, but didn't leave. ''All I'm saying is that your father is in trouble. I think you'll have a lot better shot at helping him if you know what's really going on. It won't hurt my feelings if it ends up clearing my man here, but the bottom line for you is that ignorance isn't bliss. Do yourself a favor. Join the team. In the end, it might save your old man's life.''

He went back into his pocket and tossed a couple of twenties at Max. ''Eat something. You look like hell. The car's by the north exit. Call me tomorrow night. Maybe I'll have something for you by then.''

Max didn't say anything as Peter headed toward the exit. What could he say? Thanks for risking your career? Your life?

''Let me out, Max. It's over. I'm not convinced.''

''You have absolutely no doubt in your mind.''

She met his gaze and he had his answer. She could deny the seed of doubt he and Peter had planted, but it was there in her fearful green eyes.

She softly cleared her throat. ''I can't say I won't do some digging into my father's affairs. But I honestly don't expect to find anything amiss.''

"I'll walk you out." Max stood, pocketed the money, then stepped aside to let her up. They moved out of the way of a party of four who rushed for the table, and then they headed for the entrance.

As they forced their way through the mob waiting for tables, Max suddenly felt something hard poke him in the back. As he reached to see what it was, a voice stopped him.

"Put your hand in your pocket and walk naturally, Mr. Travis, or I'll kill you where you stand."

Jade heard and turned her head, startled.

"You too, Ms. Parker."

She tried to get a look at the guy but he was bundled up, a hood covering half his face. She swallowed her fear. "You've mistaken me for someone else."

"Do you have any idea what a nine millimeter exit wound looks like? It's not pretty. Let's just stroll to your car. Walk normally."

"You're making a mistake."

"Shut up, Ms. Parker. Don't speak again."

Jade's mind raced. It was sunny but cold, in a busy parking lot, and she was being forced along by a man with a gun. Suddenly, being kidnapped by Max didn't seem so bad. She saw her car not far ahead.

"You drive," the man said to her. "Max and I will sit in back."

"Here," Max said. He pulled Peter's keys from his pocket.

She looked at him, and something in his eyes told her to go along with him. She reached for the keys and he dropped them to the pavement. She looked at their abductor.

"Pick them up." He gave her a smile that bore no

humor and she noted his silver crown. No one got silver crowns anymore. Who the hell was this guy? He motioned with the gun in his coat pocket. She bent to comply.

Max swung about with his left fist, his full weight behind it, catching the taller man full on the chin. The man fell back against the Lincoln with a grunt, involuntarily pulling the trigger of his gun, and the sharp report rang in the parking lot as a small hole appeared in his coat pocket.

Max leaped on him and grabbed the man's right wrist with both hands as he struggled to pull the gun out. He hit Max ineffectively on the back with his left fist and Max kneed him in the groin.

Another shot, and Max grunted, one hand going to his left side. He let loose with his right hand and slammed the man across the nose with his fist and was rewarded with a crack of cartilage and a spray of blood.

As the man fell sideways, Max still holding his right wrist, his coat pocket tore away and he lifted the gun as a business card fluttered to the ground next to Peter's keys. Max pushed the man's hand as high as he could, so the gun was aiming at the sky, and kneed him again. The gun fell to the ground, and Max kicked it beneath the car.

"Jade. Grab the keys."

She nodded and bent, picking up the keys and the card as the man fell, gagging and clutching his stomach. She stood, and Max kicked him again with all his might, then grabbed her arm and ran toward the north end of the lot.

The crowd had turned toward the noise, and Max

yelled, ''Gun. Man with a gun,'' pointing back to where the man was crawling under Jade's car to retrieve his weapon. Several people pulled out cell phones.

Max pointed at a silver Taurus. ''That's Pete's.'' They ran toward it. Jade started around to the passenger side, but Max stopped her with a touch. He handed her the keys. ''I'm afraid you're going to have to drive,'' he said.

She noticed the side of his coat was soaked with blood. Her stomach turned, but there was no time for squeamishness now. She opened the driver's side, leaning over to unlock the door for him. The car started as he climbed in and lay back against the headrest, and she gunned it, glad there was no snow under the tires.

They fishtailed out onto the street, slowing when she saw the police cars arriving, sirens wailing and red lights flashing. She caught her breath and forced herself to calm down as she drove for the highway at legal speeds.

''Damn you,'' she said, looking over at Max. ''He knew me. He could have killed me. What the hell did you get me into?''

Max didn't answer. His body lolled forward against the seat belt.

Chapter Six

"Max. Wake up, Max."

He stirred, the shoulder strap of the seat belt pressing tightly across his chest. He groaned as pain turned his stomach.

"C'mon, Max. Where do I turn?"

The blackness slid from his sight to be replaced with the white of snow. He shook his head to clear it, but the pain made him stop.

"Max. Please."

Cautiously, he turned his head toward Jade. Her attention was split between the narrow country lane and him. "The turnoff, Max. I don't know where the turnoff is."

He blinked twice and focused his attention on his surroundings. Observant woman. She'd managed to get them to the road that led to the cabin. Blearily, he sorted out the landmarks they passed. "About half a mile. On the right. A dirt road. You should see our tracks."

She spotted it and made the right, slowing considerably when Max moaned sharply as she went over the first bump. As she drove, following their earlier tracks back, she shut out his little hisses of pain. The only way she could slow more would be to stop, and she didn't dare do that.

The trail seemed longer going in than out, but then she'd been a passenger on her way to freedom. Now she was—what? Not exactly a fugitive. A kidnap victim, who hadn't done one thing wrong. On the other hand, the man with the silver tooth obviously knew her and had been prepared to shoot her.

She sighed. The sky threatened to drop more snow, and the light barely penetrated the pregnant clouds. Although she probably didn't need them, she turned on the headlights.

There. Through the next copse of trees. She saw the outline of the cabin, and for the tenth time wondered if she were doing the right thing. Maybe she should have driven Max straight to a hospital. No telling how serious the wound was and whether she'd be able to tend to him. But if she did that, he'd be captured.

She stopped in front of the garage door and exited with a glance at Max. He'd passed out again a mile or so back, but his breathing seemed steady. She opened the garage door and climbed back in, then pulled the car inside.

After she'd closed the garage and found the light, she turned her attention to getting him inside.

As she leaned across him to undo his seat belt, she became sickeningly aware of the sharp tang of blood. The clasp came loose and his body fell forward. It was all she could do to push him back upright. "Max. Come on, I can't carry you."

He moaned, opened his eyes without focusing.

"Come on, swing your feet around."

With her help, he did. She tugged him to his feet with his arm across her shoulder and half-carried him through the door to the interior of the cabin. She got him to the bed and dropped him on it with his legs hanging off the edge. Max groaned once, then passed out, falling back so his head just missed the pillow.

She turned up the heater, then moved to the bags Max had dumped on the counter that morning. She'd told him to get a first-aid kit, and she hoped he'd done so.

He had. It was a large kit, bigger than she'd hoped for, and she opened it. It had a number of small gauze pads, and several larger ones, along with some sterile wipes. She grabbed the pads, the wipes, and the adhesive tape.

The heater pumped out warm air, but it would be a long time before the enclosed space was comfortable. Jade removed her coat, then washed her hands. She went across the room to Max's motionless body.

No prude, Jade had undressed a man before, but never one so inert. Unsure of how to proceed, she began by removing his blood-soaked coat. It took her a long time and she was sweating by the time it hit the floor. With that gone, she was able to see that the wound under his shirt was still oozing, so she ran and got a couple of towels from the bathroom and slipped one under him as best she could before struggling to lift him enough to remove his shirt.

Undoing the buttons only went so far. She had to search the kitchen drawers until she found scissors and then it took another long time to cut away the material.

He moaned as she dropped him back on the bed, unable to hold him up any longer, and she was glad to see even this sign of life. His color seemed better to her, too. Thank God Max took care of himself, because he'd need all the help he could get. She was no doctor, didn't even like to watch medical shows.

Her gaze went to his wound. Two wounds, actually. The shot had gone completely through his body on the left side. Silently she prayed it hadn't hit anything vital. Since the hole in his back seemed to have bled the most, she rolled him over, determined to treat the worst part first.

It only took one of the antiseptic swabs for her to realize there wouldn't be enough of them to clean him up completely. She got a bowl from the kitchenette and ran the water until it was too hot for her to put her fingers in and filled the bowl, then got another towel from the bathroom and hurried back to him.

Using the towel and hot water, she cleaned the wound as best she could, using another antiseptic wipe at the end, then taped a pair of gauze pads over the still oozing wound.

Fortunately, it looked like the worst of the bleeding was over. Unfortunately, from the condition of his shirt and coat, he'd lost a lot of blood. She rolled him onto his back again. She cleaned the wound on the front, getting the cloth of his coat and shirt out, then used an antiseptic swab to finish up. She taped gauze across that wound, then went to work getting the rest of his clothes off.

His shoes and socks were no problem, but his pants were something else. After she undid his belt and the button, she paused, unaccountably embarrassed. She looked at Max's face. He was still unconscious. Pale as a ghost. She unzipped his pants and pulled them down across his hips, then moved to the foot of the bed and grabbed the legs and jerked, then again, finally sliding his denims off his feet. He wore boxers. Blue. At least where they weren't soaked with blood.

She glanced quickly at his face again, then his chest. He looked peaceful, as if he was sleeping. His chest rose and fell in a steady, even rhythm. Finally, her gaze moved down to the patch job she'd done. Except for the blood that had soaked the comforter, it didn't look too awful. But the shorts had to go. After tugging them down past his belly button, she got the scissors and cut them straight up both sides. She hesitated before pulling the top down, but then realized she was being ridiculous. Which didn't stop her from staring at him once she'd pulled the underwear clear.

Dark hair, nicely proportioned. Funny how it looked so vulnerable when it was…resting. Her gaze moved up to his belly. The slim line of hair leading up to his chest.

With a jolt, she realized what she'd just done. That she'd saved his life. Her kidnapper's life. No. Max's life. Her perception of him had changed. A lot. Maybe it was the fact that he'd called the police about the man with the license plates. Or the way Peter had looked at him. Or perhaps it was the fact that he'd been willing to let her go, at such a great personal cost.

She just wished she'd been able to contact her father. At least he knew she was alive, thanks to Max. That had to be some comfort to him.

She had to wonder, though, if her father had made the connection between Max Travis and Geotech. If he understood the stakes. He probably had no idea he was the subject of such scrutiny.

Her gaze focused once more on Max, although this time dispassionately, as if she were taking notes for a class. His body was fine, aesthetically pleasing in every way. Except for the hole in him. The wound that might get infected, might kill him. She would do her best to see that he didn't die. Because they had work to do. Both of them.

She pulled the comforter, stained with his blood, out from under his inert body, then covered him carefully.

He seemed to be resting comfortably, and she had no idea what else she could do. If he didn't make it through the night, well, she'd face that in the morning. What really scared her was the loss of blood. How much would it take to be fatal?

She turned the TV on, paced, unable to sit still, then changed the channel. There were only three. No news was on.

As she went to turn on the lights, she decided a cup of coffee would serve her well, and she fired up the coffee pot, then went to look out the window as the coffee began to bubble down. The dark skies looked threatening. Something else to worry about. Would the car be able to make it out if there were more snow? Did Peter have all-weather tires? Chains?

She stuck her hand in her pocket and felt something. The card she'd picked up after that bastard had tried to kill her.

She pulled it out and looked at it, back first. Written

in a precise script was the word "Theodore's" and the address in Arlington. Curious, she flipped the card over.

It was an expensive business card, as those things go, done in an embossed script. Belonging to a C. J. Harris, with a phone number. And right in the center, the easily recognizable Geotech logo.

Her hand shook as she set the coffee cup on the desk. She stared at the TV, trying to sort out her thoughts and emotions. Just because Max appeared to be right about Geotech, it still didn't mean her father had done anything wrong. Or that he hadn't been forced to do something—

The sound of her name made her spin toward the television.

The lead story on the news was the sighting of Max and herself in Theodore's parking lot. Shots had been reported, but no body was found, although her car had been towed to the FBI lab. Senator Parker offered a terse "no comment" when asked what his daughter might be doing, then there was a recap of the Max Travis case. Her father had looked like hell. Dark circles blemished his eyes and his suit was wrinkled, but worse, much worse, was the desperation in his voice, in his posture. He was scared to death because of her.

She turned the TV off and sat in the pool of light. She hadn't felt this frightened and lonely since the orphanage.

There had to be a way to work this out. To exonerate Max, to find out what Geotech was up to, to find the bastard that had tried to kill them. She knew if her father had a clear understanding of the situation, he could set it straight. Make things right. Assure her that he'd done nothing wrong.

She sighed. Maybe a shower. She plucked the bathrobe from the pile of clothes he'd purchased—God, was it only this morning?—and headed for the comfort of steam and hot water.

Afterward, she put on the granny nightgown he'd bought and found the soft flannel oddly comforting. Although in another life it was barely dinnertime, she turned the light out and crawled under the covers with Max, grateful to find him still alive.

SHE AWOKE WITH a start, swimming up from a deep dark sleep into the misty gray of early morning. Her dreams had been disjointed and troubling, and she pushed them from her mind and blinked several times, taking in her surroundings.

She was cuddled tightly to Max, her arm across his chest. Gently she pulled back and rested on her elbow and willed her eyes to pick out his features in the dawn glow. He didn't seem so pale, although it was hard to tell, and his breathing was even and natural. She touched his chest gently, feeling for his heartbeat, and it was slow but strong.

She moved her hand down to feel the gauze and found instead that she'd overshot and touched something quite different. She jerked her hand away and her face flushed so heavily she felt she was glowing in the dimness. Well, his blood pressure was fine, that was for sure.

She gently got out of bed and headed for the kitchenette, where she got the coffee pot going, then into the bathroom to brush her teeth.

When she emerged, Max was awake.

"That sure smells good."

The mere sound of his voice flooded her with so much relief and emotion she almost started crying. "How're you feeling?" she asked, as shc busied herself with pouring his coffee.

"Like I was shot in the side and saved by an angel."

"Hah. I'm no angel, and I'm certainly not the one who attacked the man with the gun." She brought the coffee to the bed and watched him struggle to sit up. "Can you make it?"

"I think so." She propped a pair of pillows against the wall and helped him sit up enough up to lean against them. She sat on the edge of the bed and handed him the steaming cup.

"Thanks." He sipped. "I can't help but notice that I'm not wearing pajamas."

"You lost a lot of blood. Hope you've got another coat. I had to get that stuff off you to dress your wounds."

"Guess I bled on my pants, too?"

"Yeah, you had no sense of decorum."

"Ah. I'm like that when I'm wounded." He smiled, but it was cut short the minute he moved. "Could you get me something to put on? I've really got to get to the bathroom."

"Do you have a robe?"

"No, but there's a coat in the closet."

She found the coat and brought it back to him, then helped him as he tried to get it on while sitting. His pain was obvious. "Max. You may have to forego modesty to get out of bed."

He frowned.

"It's not like I've never seen it."

"Hell, I don't care about that. It's the stiffness."

She put her hand up to hide her laugh.

"I'm glad I amuse you."

"You do. In all sorts of ways." She held out her hand. "C'mon, I'll help you."

With her assistance, he sat up, but standing was a bit trickier. After one false start, he sat back down hard, and his curse said all she needed to know about the pain.

"You can do it." Jade stood in front of him and held out both hands, and Max grabbed them and she pulled him to his feet. He was very shaky, and she positioned herself beside him, lifting his hand across her shoulders and walked him to the bathroom. "Will you be all right?"

"It's not like I have a choice. I'll pound on the wall if anything goes wrong."

"Okay." She paced the cabin until he emerged, the coat now buttoned. He'd made an attempt to comb his hair and didn't look half-bad, other than tottering like a drunk and occasionally falling with his shoulder against a wall.

"You've lost a lot of blood, Max. Why don't you lie back down and let me get you some food."

He swayed unevenly in the kitchenette and finally nodded. He made it to the bed and crawled in, still wrapped in the coat.

Jade found a can of chicken noodle soup in the groceries he'd brought and quickly opened it and poured it into a saucepan. "After you eat, I'm going to change those bandages."

"Yeah," he said, his voice unnaturally soft. "We have to talk about yesterday."

"What about it?"

He hesitated, and she glanced over her shoulder at him. His hooded gaze tracked her movements as she stirred the soup and got down a bowl.

"Are you pretty sure we weren't followed?" he asked, finally.

"No way. It's been almost twenty-four hours."

"I've been out that long?"

"Yep."

After another brief silence, he asked, "Why did you do it?"

"Do what?"

"Help me."

"You were hurt." She looked at him. Their eyes met and a shiver slid down her spine. "For God's sake, did you think I'd leave you there?"

"You know what I mean. You could have turned me over to the police."

She sighed and turned her attention back to the soup. Damn, she should have anticipated the question. "I don't know."

Fortunately, he backed off and she finished in silence, her brain a jumble of thoughts, none of them making sense.

When the soup was hot, she poured some into a cup and carried it over to him. He was asleep. She stood there, staring at him, the way his lips parted ever so slightly, the innocent way his lashes lay on his pale cheeks, and she realized she wanted very much to believe him. Not that her father was corrupt, but that Max had been set up.

"Max, wake up. Eat this."

He blinked awake and took the cup. After a few sips, his eyelids sagged and Jade took the cup from him.

She smiled sadly. "We gotta check those bandages."

He nodded, and she helped him get the coat off.

"Back one first," she said.

It took him a minute to roll onto his stomach. Jade dressed the wound again, encouraged by the healthy clotting and lack of anything too dark and scary. Thank goodness for *E.R.* She even knew enough to sniff to make sure there was no necrosis. "Okay, roll over."

He didn't move. Her heart leaped until she realized he was only asleep again.

She rolled him over, dressed the front wound, and then pulled the covers up to his chin.

She paced the small cabin, got more coffee, and looked out the window. Her gaze stopped at the laptop and the stack of papers. Sighing, she picked up the bundle and put them on the desk. Once again, she started reading.

Although she'd skimmed through pieces of the stack before, this time she read carefully, which took a lot longer. By the time she looked up again, it was mid-afternoon, and the clock that cued her was her stomach.

She pushed the desk chair aside, checked on the still-sleeping Max, and fixed herself a tuna sandwich. But she couldn't eat it. She just watched him as he slept, grateful for his even breathing and troubled about all she'd read. Not just troubled, but sick to her stomach.

Maybe the same person who'd framed Max had framed her father. Made it look like he was in bed with Geotech. God, she needed fresh air. She got rid of the uneaten sandwich, pulled on her coat and stepped outside.

The air was crisp and cold. The smell of pine and snow tickled her nose even as the information she was absorbing gnawed at her brain. After several deep breaths, she picked a large tree in the distance and headed for it, lifting her feet carefully to wade through the snow. The hiking shoes Max had bought worked well, the treads provided a good grip, and the high tops kept snow from getting to her ankles.

Winded, she reached the tree and turned about, looking at her tracks and the cabin in the near distance.

She could see this would be a great place to relax, get away for a weekend. Something she never did. She'd been something of a bookworm in college, then started working for her father in the high-pressure position of executive assistant, while studying for her Ph.D.

Even her vacations had been of the ''If this is Tuesday, it must be Belgium'' variety, whirlwinds of stops with little chance to really become familiar with the area or the people. This little cabin, the surrounding forest—there was a peace here she'd long lacked.

Shaking her head, she headed back for the cabin, hardly believing all that had happened in the last few days. Being kidnapped was bad enough, but those moments when that bastard had tried to kill them had shortened her life by a good week. She shivered, and not from the cold.

But none of it was half as bad as the sick feeling in her gut from the material she'd read, although she still believed with all her heart that her father wasn't the bad guy Max thought he was. There was still a lot more to read, and she felt sure once she had all the pieces put together, there would be a perfectly reasonable explanation for his change of heart regarding the energy company.

As darkness fell, she woke Max briefly and helped him drink almost a half cup of soup. He dozed through the changing of the bandages and was asleep as she pulled the covers up to his neck.

She tried watching TV, but except for a brief piece on her kidnapping, couldn't find anything that caught her interest. Again, the sight of her father, looking worse by the day, depressed her beyond measure. By nine, physical and emotional stress had exhausted her and she crawled into bed with Max again. His body warmed her instantly, and it felt like the most natural thing in the world to let her hand run down the length of his back. To press her thigh against his hip. He barely stirred.

She woke just after seven, and went through the same routine. In fact, the whole morning was a repeat of the day before until after she took her walk. This time, when she returned, Max stirred.

"Well, sleeping beauty."

His lips lifting slightly, he ran a hand through his thoroughly rumpled hair. "Give me a hand with the coat, would you?"

"Sure." She knelt on the bed and helped him get the coat wrapped around him, then helped him up.

"I'm going to try to make it on my own."

"You sure?"

"No." He grinned weakly at her. "But I feel like I've been sleeping my life away."

"I'll stay close, just in case."

He nodded and shuffled toward the bathroom. Once he was safely in, Jade put on a new pot of coffee and heated up more soup.

"That smells great."

She turned to find Max standing by the bathroom door. He'd brushed his teeth and hair, and if it wasn't for his pallor and the dark smudges under his eyes, he would have looked pretty good.

"You look like a flasher."

He waggled his eyebrows. "Want some candy, little girl?"

"Santa suits, baseball caps, overcoats. You like playing dress-up, don't you? Admit it."

"Yeah, right." He looked down at the coat. "Speaking of which..."

"Just your pajamas, okay? They'll be easy for me to get into."

His brows rising, he laughed, and then groaned and touched his side.

"See? You got punished for having your mind in the gutter. I should make you change your own bandages."

"Okay, I give." His attention shifted toward the coffee pot. "Mmm. The nectar of the Gods."

"Not the way I make it."

He smiled at her, something soft and sweet about

his tired eyes, then tottered to his pajamas. She heard his slow shuffle, then the bathroom door closed once more.

By the time he came out, she'd set the table and dumped another can of soup in the pan. This time, however, she'd doctored the canned soup with some thinly sliced celery and carrot, wishing she had some green onions to add to the mix.

"Have you ever thought about how weird pajamas are?" Max said, startling her. He moved toward the table, his gait a bit more stable than it had been yesterday, although he wouldn't be running any marathons soon.

"How do you mean?"

"Well, look." Max motioned to the breast pocket. "As if you're going to go to bed with, what, a pack of cigarettes in your pocket? A pen holder? Why don't they have a little flannel vest?"

Jade laughed out loud. "Take those aspirin first, then try like hell to finish that soup, okay? You need the protein."

"Soup? All I get is soup?"

"You were shot, Max. I probably should have taken you to a hospital."

"If you had, I'd most likely be dead now."

She sat down across from him, her own soup unappealing as dish water. "We should talk about that, Max. I've been going through your research."

He swallowed the three pills, then put the glass back on the table, his eyes watchful, hopeful.

Her gaze met his. "Overall, I think you're right. Geotech is definitely trying to influence the contract legislation."

He nodded, keeping a careful rein on his expressions.

"And they're definitely not above murder. The guy who shot you dropped a Geotech card with the name of that coffee shop on the back."

Max had picked up his spoon, but promptly dropped it. "Jesus. That means they've got Peter's phone tapped. I've got to warn him."

She put a gentling hand on his arm. "Tomorrow, Max. If you keel over now, you're finished. I'll drive into town tomorrow."

"Tell him..."

"I'll warn him. Don't worry. I've worked in government for years."

"I should never have gotten him involved." He stared blindly at his untouched soup, and then raised his gaze to her. "Or you."

"You were desperate. I understand. But you know how you can make it up to me?"

His brows drew together in a frown.

"Eat. You need to get your strength back."

He slowly picked up the spoon again.

They both ate quietly for several minutes. Jade knew he was worried about Peter, but she couldn't do much about that. If it was between warning his friend today and leaving Max on his own, watching out for Max won. It was still too risky to leave him alone.

"Sorry about your dad," Max said, finally.

"There's no hard proof."

"Werner said it was Senator Parker, and died bringing me the proof."

"I'll grant you're right about Geotech, but you're still wrong about Dad."

Max looked deeply into her eyes. "Jade, I know how you feel. From everything you've told me, your dad is probably a better man than most of us know. But you've got to look at the facts. It's not much of a leap to see that they were blackmailing him. The e-mails alone—"

"I'm going to prove you're wrong."

He stared at her, swallowed. "That works for me."

She blinked in surprise. "How's that?"

Max shrugged and winced from the pain. "I'm after the facts, not your father. Now, more than ever, I'd like to see you prove his involvement isn't what it seems."

She pushed her bowl away, wiped her mouth with the paper napkin. Great words, but she could tell Max didn't believe for a moment that her dad wasn't involved. "I don't want to talk about this anymore. I'll go through the rest of the stuff today."

"Jade…"

"Shut up, will you? Just shut up."

Max nodded. She could see the brief meal had taken its toll. His head bobbed and his eyelids fluttered. He stood, steadied himself with a hand on the table, then headed slowly toward the bed.

She watched him, her mind in turmoil. She'd get through the rest of Max's research this afternoon, then figure out a way to clear her father. The material Max had gathered put her father in a damning light. If it was published now, others would believe the worst. And that was not going to happen. No matter what.

Chapter Seven

While Max slept, Jade finished the papers and delved into the laptop.

The e-mails were unsettlingly incriminating. She searched for C. J. Harris, the name on the Geotech business card, and discovered the man had his finger on the pulse of everything that went on at the company. She had no doubt that whatever she'd read in e-mail was only the tip of the iceberg, carefully screened to not leave a trail. But leave a trail he had. She didn't read anything with her father's name spelled out, although there were many mentions of RP and SP. Whatever good work the company did, it was tainted now by e-mail that was too reminiscent of the Enron scandal to be left alone.

When she got home, she'd sure as hell see that a subpoena covered the server logs from Geotech's mainframe.

She sighed as she turned the laptop off. It was dark in the small cabin. She'd spent most of the afternoon poring over the rest of Max's research, and had ignored the man, only checking with brief glances to make sure he was still sleeping peacefully.

She turned the lights on. He needed to eat, and she wasn't sure he was getting everything he needed from the soup. After a quick perusal of the pantry, she found a steak in the freezer along with some brussels sprouts. That should give him a boost. He'd slept enough that she figured she could get him to eat at least part of the meal.

It felt good to busy herself in the kitchen, therapeutic. She didn't think about Geotech or her father, not even Max's wounds or the man who'd tried to kill them. Instead, she thought about her life back in Arlington.

Normally, it didn't bother her that she still lived at home with her father. The arrangement was practical, and while she'd been knee deep in school, it had been a godsend.

But in the last few months she'd been thinking a lot about moving out. Getting an apartment in Georgetown. Dating.

She wondered if she'd met Max under different circumstances, would she have been interested? Oh, yeah. Definitely. First, his looks appealed to her, and she would have been fascinated by what he did. She respected some journalists, had known a few who were bright, interesting men. There had been that one guy from Newsweek who'd asked her out. They'd attended a few social gatherings on the Hill, but then he'd gone off to Afghanistan, and she'd never heard from him again.

Max would have appealed to her, for sure, but she would have been cautious. She had to be, given her position. Along with the fascination she had for reporters, she was also suspicious of their motives. The truth was, if he'd asked her out, she probably would have said no. Because he was the kind of reporter who was always looking to dig up dirt. Boy, had he found some, but she wouldn't think about that.

She defrosted the steak in the microwave, and while that was happening, she mixed the veggies with olive oil, salt and pepper, then put them in a roasting pan and into a hot oven. Once the steak had thawed, she seasoned it and put it in a heavy saucepan.

It had been a long time since she'd been with a man she liked. A man that was suitable. So many were interested in her because of who she was, or more accurately, who her father was. Her own life, for so many years now, had been shrouded by her father's shadow. She didn't resent it, but it was a little depressing.

Just like every other woman her age, she wanted to spread her wings, fly outside the nest. But, like others in her position, there were rules, fears, obligations.

She hadn't had sex until she was nineteen. No clouds had parted, and if any angels wept, it had been out of pity. He'd been a law student who'd enticed her at a party, filled her with tepid beer and taken her virginity with such a lack of finesse that she'd wondered, for a hell of a long time, what all the fuss was about.

Two years ago, she'd been enlightened by an older man, an art dealer from Paris, who'd given her a few lessons in the art of making love. The relationship had gone nowhere, but her hopes had come back to life. Somewhere out there might just be a man who could interest her mind and excite her body.

The biggest thrill she'd gotten since then was getting a peek at Max's naked body. How sad was that?

She turned the steak, shook the sprouts in the oven.

How inappropriate was it to be thinking X-rated thoughts about her kidnapper? She should be ashamed. But she wasn't. She was intrigued by the man. Unfortunately, unless he could come up with some pretty powerful magic, he was going to be in jail for a long time.

If he wasn't dead.

The thought shook her to the core. Damn, how could she care so much? She didn't know him. Not really. But damn it, she did care and she'd help him get well, and then she'd help him see that her father wasn't the bad guy Max thought he was. Help the authorities see that Max wasn't a killer. And she'd do everything in her power to take down Geotech, and find the man with the silver tooth.

While the steak finished cooking, she gathered her first aid supplies and put them by the bed. Max snored. Not loudly, but she heard it when she was close. Stupidly, it made her weepy, which probably said more about her lack of sleep and the tension she'd been under than anything else.

She hurried back to the kitchen and put the finishing touches on the meal.

She used a cutting board as a tray and took the food along with silverware, a napkin, water and some aspirin. This should help on his road to recovery. At least she hoped so.

Max's eyes fluttered as her weight dipped the side of the bed. She put the food aside and picked up the gauze and the water. ‘‘Time to change the bandages, Max.’’

His eyes and voice heavy with sleep, he asked, ‘‘You sure?’’

‘‘All I know about medicine I learned on TV. The Girl Scouts didn’t cover gunshot wounds.’’

‘‘I bet you’d make a great doctor.’’ He smiled at her, although he looked a bit loopy, which made her think he wasn’t fully alert.

‘‘Thankfully, I’m not squeamish. But I don’t have the kind of dedication you’d need to be a doctor.’’

‘‘I don’t know. You managed to work and get your doctorate at the same time. That’s pretty damn dedicated.’’

‘‘Yeah, yeah, I’m Supergirl. Now get that top off and roll over.’’

‘‘Jeez. You sure need work on your bedside manner.’’ He pulled the pajama top off and lay on his stomach.

Jade examined the gauze. The back wound was still oozing, but only slightly. She dipped a towel in the hot water and soaked the gauze. ‘‘You want it fast or slow?’’

‘‘Take your—yow.’’

His yelp was in response to her pulling the tape off in one pull. ‘‘It’s actually more painful to do it slow.’’

‘‘You could’ve fooled me.’’

She bent to clean the area, ignoring his occasional twitch. When she was done, she wrapped him back up, pretty as a Christmas present. ‘‘Okay. Turn over.’’

He did so, slowly, and she redressed the wound on the front. She couldn’t help but notice that Max was aroused by her touch. ''Feeling a little frisky, are we?''

The blush she expected didn't come. Instead, his once sleepy grin became wolfish and his gaze wasn't dreamy whatsoever. ''Not a lot I can do about it, unfortunately.''

''Hmm. What was that famous Shakespeare quotation? 'As if?'''

He laughed. ''Don't worry. Your virtue is completely safe.''

''I'll say. You can hardly pee by yourself.'' She patted him just below the bandage, but above the tent pole.

He grabbed her hand, more tightly than she ever would have guessed. ''I won't be laid up forever.''

She smiled brightly, hiding the quick flutter that hit her belly. ''You will be if I kill you.''

He didn't let go right away, but his grip eased. He rubbed his thumb on the thin, tender skin of her inner wrist. ''I've gotten you into a hell of a mess, haven't I?''

She slipped her hand from his. Wrapped her arms around her waist. ''Go to sleep. You have a lot to do, and you can't do it on your back.''

Amusement twinkled in his eyes as he looked over at the food she'd set aside. ''Don't I get to eat?''

She mentally cringed, annoyed at how much he'd disconcerted her. Calmly, she moved the tray to a spot on the bed in front of him.

''Aren't you going to join me?''

Shaking her head, she backed away. ''I've got something else I've gotta do.''

Ignoring his concerned look, she went to the couch

and wrapped herself in a blanket and stared outside at the snow. For a long time, she simply thought. About her life. What she wanted. What the hell she was going to do next.

SHE WOKE IN the cold gray of dawn, in bed with Max, her sleep having been a mixed blessing. She'd had unwelcome dreams of Max, dreams that featured him without pajamas and her with flannel nightgown pushed up around her waist, and good lord, he seemed awfully healthy.

She pushed herself into the chill of the cabin.

Max didn't move. He could've been in a coma, his sleep was so deep, but she watched him carefully and saw the steady rise and fall of his chest. His color seemed better, so she wasn't terribly worried.

She dressed quickly and heated some coffee. As she gulped it down, she looked up Peter's work number on the laptop. After leaving a note for Max right next to some more aspirin and a glass of water, she took her cup, grabbed her coat and headed out to Peter's car.

Nearly forty-five minutes later, she pulled up at the phone booth she'd shared with Max. It started snowing as she turned off the car, so she got her change together quickly and headed off to phone Peter.

"Peter Shelby."

"Go to another phone and call this number." She read the number of the phone booth. "I'll wait five minutes. Do it now."

"But..."

She hung up and then stood in the booth watching

traffic go by, keeping her head down so that no one could recognize her. The idea that the silver-toothed man was out there hunting them was far more unsettling than it had been back at the cabin.

The phone rang and she lifted the receiver. ''Hello?''

''Ms. Parker?''

''Your work phone is tapped, Peter. Max wanted you to know. He said to tell you to be careful what you say.''

''Christ, is he okay? I heard about the shooting.''

''He'll be fine. He was shot, but it's not serious.''

''The police didn't know if anyone had been hit, although they found blood. What about you? You okay?''

''Yes. I'm taking care of Max.'' She glanced around, but no one was in sight. ''Look, I've got to get back to him, but he wanted you to know about the phone tap.''

''Man. They've got some juice to tap a phone at the paper.'' There were traffic sounds behind him. ''Okay, Ms. Parker. Can you relay a message to him?''

''Of course.''

''Tell him I'm going to talk to Patti Gellar, and Mrs. Edwards. Werner had a computer at home, and I might be able to get her to let me look at it. It'll probably take me another day or so. Also, I found the name of that Cayman account.''

''Okay. You want to give me the name?''

She felt a hesitation even over the wire, but finally he said, ''Geotech transferred half a million dollars into an account with the password 'Princess Pea.'''

She didn't say anything for a moment. Couldn't. But then she cleared her voice if not her head. "I'll tell him, Peter. Be careful. Don't use the phone. And watch your back."

"You, too. Tell him to call when he's feeling better. Have him say he's Frank."

"I will."

"And Ms. Parker? Max is a straight-up guy. Maybe the most honorable man I know. He didn't kill anyone."

"I know. We'll get him out of this."

"I sure as hell hope so. You be careful."

She said goodbye and hung up, still thinking about what Peter had said. Instead of heading right back to the cabin, she drove through the town until she saw the small department store.

Fifteen minutes later, she and her package were back in the car. Luckily, it was a light, powdery snowfall, but still, she made her way carefully, hoping Max was all right. Hoping for lots of things.

She entered to find Max sitting uncomfortably at the table wrapped in the long coat.

"I was worried," he said.

"I called Peter." She set the department store bag on the table. "And I brought you a gift. Maybe it'll pay you back for these." She looked down at the jeans, shoes and shirt he'd bought her.

As Max pulled the robe from the bag, he asked, "What did Peter have to say?"

"I got him to call me from another phone, then told him his work phone was tapped. He said he was going to talk to someone named Patti Gellar, but wants to talk to you first. And Mrs. Edwards." She poured herself a cup of coffee and sat down across from Max. The warmth from the cup helped with her hands, but did nothing for her frozen feet.

"Did he say when?"

She shook her head. "I assume Mrs. Edwards is Werner's wife. Who's Patti Gellar?"

"Werner's secretary." Max looked off with a worried frown.

"What's wrong?"

"After what happened to us, I'm not sure involving Mrs. Edwards or Patti is wise."

"Hell, Max, it's nice that you're concerned, but you can't turn your nose up at any lead. They may have something you need."

"You're right." He didn't look convinced. "Thanks for this," Max said, holding the robe up and looking at it. He slipped the coat off, exposing the fact that he was wearing only the pajama bottoms, and slipped the robe on. "Nice." He sat back down. "Is that all he said?"

She hesitated, really hating this part. But whether she told him or not, he'd find out eventually. "He found the name of the Cayman account you were looking for."

"Well? What is it?"

She looked at the empty bag still on the table. "Princess Pea."

When she looked up again, Max looked puzzled. "Princess Pea? What the hell does that mean? Damn." He stared into his coffee cup as though there were tea leaves at the bottom.

"You know, Max, when I was a kid, I had a kitten.'' She pushed a spoon around the table like a chess piece.

He didn't say anything. Just watched her.

''I bet if you try real hard, you can guess her name.''

''I see.''

''They could have gotten the name, somehow. Used it as part of their blackmail.''

Max nodded, but she could tell he wasn't buying it.

''My father wouldn't be involved in murder.'' She got up and walked to the window. ''He's not like that.''

Max rose with a muffled moan, then came slowly behind her. ''Jade…''

She stared at nothing. The landscape that had seemed quaint a few hours ago now was bleak and full of dead things. ''Ever since I was little, Dad made a point of spending my birthday with me. Decades of birthdays.'' She felt so weary she had to brace her hand on the windowsill. ''Not my last one.''

Max put his broad hands on her shoulders. ''There's an explanation,'' he said. ''We'll find it. Together.''

She turned suddenly and buried her face in his chest, sobbing, her hands balled into fists between them.

Max hardly knew what to do, except the obvious. He put his arms around her, held her tight, murmured soothing words. Felt pangs of guilt at the pleasure he took from the scent of her hair.

After awhile, her crying faded. The hard balls of her fists relaxed, her hands opened, her palms pressed against his chest. Her breathing quickened, deepened.

Max felt the change on a molecular level, and the way he held her had little to do with comfort. He could feel the heat from her body penetrating even the thick robe, and his flesh responded. Blood swept to his groin, answering heat with heat, and a low moan rose in his throat.

She raised her head and her gaze found his. Everything shifted. The night, the air. The heat.

He bent his head to hers and their lips touched.

Jade heard a small animal sound, and knew that it was rising from her own throat. A spark kindled between her legs, sending fire into her belly, and she moved her arms to embrace him, pulling him as close as she could, which wasn't nearly close enough.

She pulled her lips away, losing herself in his eyes before she pushed against him again, lips pressing, tongues probing, the swelling firmness of him answering her own wetness.

He pulled back, gasped, but not from pleasure.

"Oh, God. I've hurt you."

He closed his eyes, pressed a hand to the front bandage. He'd paled, and she wished she had the strength to carry him to bed.

"I'm sorry. Oh, damn it, I'm such an idiot." She touched his shoulder, eased him toward the bed. "Come on. Take it slow."

He didn't argue, just took one small step after another.

She took the robe from him, pulled back the covers, then lent her arm so he could lean on her as he lowered himself between the sheets.

She breathed again once he was safely under covers, but she didn't move. Not an inch. She simply watched him. It took several minutes, but his breathing grew normal, the pink came back to his skin. He even smiled.

"Sorry," he said.

"Not your fault."

"Can I have a rain check?"

Heat filled her cheeks, but she didn't turn away. "I'd like that."

His eyes fluttered closed. "Good," he whispered.

"TELL ME ABOUT Patti Gellar."

Max was at the table again, sipping tea while Jade whipped up dinner. He forced himself not to wince as he drank. She'd been so pleased with herself for finding the herb tea that he hadn't had the heart to tell her he hated the stuff. Found it a lot like drinking swamp water. "She's Werner's secretary. She'd been with him for over twenty years."

"I know she's his secretary. I want to know if she's someone we should consider being in cahoots with Geotech."

"No, oh no. Werner and Patti were sort of like Perry Mason and Della Street. Patti could never betray Werner much less be involved in his murder." He took one long drink of the tepid liquid, preferring one powerful shudder to a series of small quakes. Then he pushed the cup away. Still, he hadn't finished the vile stuff. He planned to wait until Jade went to the bathroom, then find the tea and throw it out the window.

"I'm not saying she was involved in his murder,

or anything else. But maybe she was duped like my father.''

Max said nothing. Didn't even look at her in case she noticed pity in his eyes. When it came to her father, she was so damn naive. ''I think our next step is to get into Werner's computer.''

''What about this *Irish Mist* thing? And Silver Tooth?''

''I'm hoping Herb—my contact at the FBI—can come up with something.''

''Can you trust him?''

Max shrugged, which wasn't all that wise. ''I think so, but I could end up dead wrong. At this point, my options are limited.''

She came to the table bearing a big bowl of pasta and a smaller bowl of salad. ''Eat,'' she said, as she doled him out way too large a portion of spaghetti. ''Before computers, before anything, you have to be mobile.''

''I'm better. And I'll be better still if I can shower tonight.''

She sat down, her expression forecasting her dubiousness about his plan.

''Hey, you can join me. Make sure I don't slip and fall.''

She ducked her head as she made a job of unfolding her napkin. ''Tell you what. I'll stand outside. You make it quick.''

He ate a forkful of the pasta, enjoying food for the first time in days. Or maybe it was the prospect of the shower that cheered him up. ''I think it would be much safer if you were in the shower with me.''

Jade looked at him. "Hmm. And here I'd assumed our first shower together would be anything but safe."

He coughed so hard he had to finish the damn tea.

IT WAS TEN FIFTEEN, and Max had been sleeping for two hours. He'd showered, which had both cheered him up and exhausted him. But she could tell he was healing. His color was much better, his slow shuffle wasn't quite as slow, and he certainly had more of his wits about him. He'd even called to her from the bathroom to come dry his back. She almost had, but thought better of it. The man was sick. And since that kiss, things between them had changed.

At least for her.

She turned off his laptop, more discouraged than ever, then she shut off the television. It was her turn to shower, but first she went to the bed, touched Max's forehead. He wasn't clammy any longer, and he had no fever. In fact, if she hadn't known, she never would have suspected he'd been shot. She thanked the gods for guiding that shot to the very edge of his side, to a space that had no vital organs or major arteries. All in all, they'd been lucky, although she doubted Max would agree.

After getting her nightgown and slippers, she went into the bathroom and closed the door. They were down to one towel now, the only one not stained with his blood. It was still slightly damp, but there was nothing she could do about that. She needed the shower, and her nightgown would get her dry.

She turned on the water, let it get hot, then stripped out of her clothes. The mirror had started to fog, but she still had a clear view of herself, naked, pale, not a lick of makeup on her face. She'd lost a little weight since this whole thing had begun, which didn't upset her much. Although she worried about not exercising.

In her real life, she worked out regularly. She took a jazzercise class at the gym, swam a few times a week, and had just started to try her hand at pilates. Exercise relaxed her, at the same time it gave her the kind of energy she needed in her frenetic life.

The small walks out to the big tree weren't cutting it. On the other hand, she'd certainly kept up her heart rate, what with being scared to death and all.

She stepped into the shower and closed her eyes as the warm water soothed her tight muscles. Her thoughts turned to Max. Not his wound, not his plight, but his kiss.

She found the soap and started lathering her body, her movements slow and languid as she remembered the feel of his lips on hers. It was nuts, but she'd never been kissed like that in her life. Not that he knew any unique techniques or even had time to experiment, but once his mouth had touched hers, she'd felt it all the way to her toes.

It was the situation, that's all. The danger. The urgency. It couldn't be anything else. Could it?

She opened her eyes and concentrated solely on getting washed. Her body, then her hair. Shaving took another few minutes, and then she was out of there, getting as dry as possible, considering, and slipping her nightgown over her head.

She brushed her teeth with fervor, shoving all thoughts of kisses right out of her mind the moment they started. Only, they kept coming back. And back.

She toweled her hair so vigorously it hurt, and it

didn't even do that much good, except to make her feel stupid. Finally, there was nothing more to do in the bath, so she took her comb and went into the main room.

Max hadn't moved an inch. She pulled a chair over to the heating vent, bent over and combed her hair, wishing she'd thought to buy a hair dryer. Next time she went to town, she would. Along with some more towels, another set of sheets. Maybe even another comforter, since theirs was so stained.

Hell, she might as well pick out her china pattern while she was at it.

The comb caught on a knot in her hair, yanking her out of the foolishness that was her mind.

"You okay?"

Jade jerked upright. "You were sleeping."

"Now I'm awake."

"Are you all right?"

"Just have to make a pit stop, then I'll be fine."

She stood. "I'll help."

"No," he said, his voice tight as he sat up. "Finish drying your hair. I can do this."

"Sure?"

He didn't answer. Instead, he stood and headed for the bathroom. He also didn't bother with the robe. Naked, except for two big gauze bandages, he walked slowly past her, not in the least embarrassed, as far as she could tell. Of course, if she'd looked at his face her assessment might have been more accurate.

He hadn't been hard. Just comfortable. All naked. Oh, dear.

She bent over again and didn't raise up when she heard him come out of the bathroom. In fact she didn't sit up until she was completely sure he was tucked back in bed.

Her hair wasn't dry, but it was close enough. If she kept this up, she was going to get good and dizzy. Besides, she was tired, and wanted to get to sleep.

She put the comb back in the bathroom, turned off the light by the table, and went to the bed. His eyes were closed, but she knew he wasn't sleeping. It didn't matter. They'd been doing this for days now. No reason to get all nervous about it now. It wasn't as if anything could happen.

After she'd taken off her slippers, she climbed into bed, making sure she and Max didn't touch at all. Not that she didn't want to. She'd become used to his warmth, comfortable with her body against his.

"Tell me what I've missed," he said.

"What do you mean?"

"I've been sleeping for days. Have we been on the news?"

"Oh," she said, rolling her eyes. She'd thought… Never mind. "Yes, we have. They haven't found us yet."

"I assume they're still looking."

"Yep. And they're all over my father."

"Ouch."

"He looks like hell, Max. It's killing him, not knowing where I am."

"I know. I think about that with my father. It sucks."

She turned to her side, looked at his profile as he lay on his back. It was dark in the room, but there must have been a full moon because she could see him pretty clearly. Not much detail, but enough to catch his frown. "You don't think there's any way to contact them? Let them know we're okay?"

"I don't see how. It might lead the feds to us, and even worse, it could put them in danger. They knew about you, Jade. That bastard was prepared to kill you."

"I know. God, it's terrifying."

He turned his head to face her. "Whoa. I didn't want to start this. I shouldn't have said a thing. You need to sleep, without nightmares."

"What?"

"You've had a couple of rough nights."

"Did I wake you?"

He nodded. "It's okay. I was glad. I was able to calm you down a bit. Let you get back to sleep."

"Did I say anything?"

"Nothing, really. But it was clear you were scared out of your wits."

"Gee, go figure."

"So let's talk about something else."

"Deal." She put her hand underneath the pillow, lifting her head a bit so she could see him better. "Tell me about you."

He smiled. "What do you want to know?"

"Everything."

He laughed. "No problem. I was conceived on a cold winter's night—"

"You know what I mean. I want to hear about your job. At least when it's not like this. Your life. I know you love your dad. What about your mom?"

"She died when I was seventeen. Cancer."

"Oh, no. God, I'm sorry. I know that pain too well."

"Yeah. She was funny. Great sense of humor. Wanted me to be a doctor."

"Not your cup of tea?"

He shook his head. "Hate blood. Especially my own."

"What got you into journalism?"

He shifted a little more toward her, and his wince seemed tamer than it had this morning. "I like to write. Got involved with my high school paper, and went from there."

"It sounds so simple. But you're with the *Washington Post.* I understand it's hard as hell to get a job there."

"I paid my dues. Did a lot of grunt work to get there."

"And you still love it?"

"When people I care about aren't in danger, yes."

"And you'll go back to it once this is over."

"Sure."

She nodded. "But with the kind of reporting you do, it might get dangerous all over again."

"Yeah. It might. But in the end, I think what I do matters."

"You sound like me."

"We're not that dissimilar. I thought about politics, but I'm not cut out for that. I don't have the patience for the b.s."

"I don't want to talk about work, either," she said. "Tell me something else. Like your love life."

"What love life?"

"You don't have someone?"

"Nope."

"You must have, though."

"Sort of."

"What does that mean?"

"It means that I've had relationships, but nothing serious."

"You've never been in love."

He shook his head.

"Why not?"

"I don't know. Busy. Focused. Peter would say obsessed."

"Have you ever come close?"

He didn't say anything for a long moment. "Close."

"Who was she?"

He smiled. "Never you mind. Now it's your turn. You ever been in love?"

"No. But I thought so at one time. He wasn't a terribly nice guy. I learned more about what I don't want from him than what I do want."

"That sounds ridiculously healthy."

"Therapy. Lots of it."

He laughed. Then she felt his hand on her shoulder. "He was an idiot."

"I know that, but how do you?"

"He didn't see you. If he had, he would have loved you the way you deserve to be loved."

She felt heat in her cheeks, and lower. A warm glow that settled deep inside her. "Thank you."

He squeezed her arm. "You're something else, Jade Parker. And while I wish we'd met under much different circumstances, I'm not at all sorry we did meet."

She smiled, couldn't help it. "Me, too."

His hand dropped. "What I want is to talk more.

Lots more. But I'm afraid my body isn't going to cooperate.''

''Sleep. Yes. You need it.''

''I'd sleep a lot better if you were closer.''

She closed her eyes, took a deep breath, then curled herself around his warmth. But she didn't sleep right away. Not while her thoughts were so caught up in a dream of an impossible tomorrow.

WITH MOST PEOPLE the size of Mr. Harris, Retik would've split them in half if they'd yelled at him like that. Reminded him of the drill sergeant in boot camp. Until he'd broken the man's arm in judo class.

Retik was fairly certain, however, that if he raised a finger to C. J. Harris's head he wouldn't leave the building alive. Perhaps not even the room. He focused his attention on the smaller man.

''...were you thinking, for God's sake? In a parking lot? It was all over the news, Retik. That's all we need.''

Discretion was the better part of valor. At least for now. Someday, he might meet Mr. Harris in a parking lot for a few minutes, but for now... ''Sorry, Mr. Harris.''

Harris walked away to look out the window, his back to Retik. ''Christ, with your record, I figured you'd have no problem with a few—clean-up operations.''

''No sir.''

Harris sat in his chair facing the desk and rubbed his brow with a well-manicured hand as though he were fighting off a headache. ''We intercepted a call to Peter Shelby. It came from a pay phone just off the highway in Virginia, so they might have headed south, but we can't take the chance. If we can't get the reporter, we've got to cut off his sources.''

''Yes, sir.''

''That traitor Edwards had a secretary. I don't think Travis has gotten to her yet, or he probably would've gone public.'' Harris gave him a look that scared half of Washington, D.C. ''Do you think you can handle an old lady, Retik?''

For a second the rage seethed in the powerfully built man, but the self-control that had kept him alive in Africa and South America served him well. ''No problem.''

''Find out what she knows, if anything. Then, for God's sake, make it look like an accident. Get it done tomorrow.'' Harris whirled the chair about in an unmistakable gesture of dismissal.

Retik ground his teeth. Someday... ''Yes, sir.''

Chapter Eight

Apprehension wasn't nearly a strong enough word. Jade paced the floor like an expectant father. ''Can't we go?''

Max sat sipping coffee. He shook his head. ''If we call too early, nobody will be there. We'd have to hang around the phone booth.''

''But—''

''Calm down, Jade. Have more coffee.''

The dichotomy of the requests didn't escape her, but she poured herself another cup and sat. Max looked a hell of a lot better. He'd showered and shaved, and his hair was combed. If she met him at, say, an embassy ball, she'd definitely be impressed. She wondered how he'd look in tails.

Her gaze drifted to the gun lying on the table and she shivered. There was no mistaking the single lethal purpose for which the device was intended; to deliver a half-ounce of lead to a living creature and render it dead. To say she was not fond of guns would be an understatement. ''Do we have to take—that?''

Max nodded. ''If we run into Silver Tooth again, I

might not be so lucky. Did you see the size of that guy?"

"Lucky? I thought you handled him pretty well. Except for the getting shot part."

"I caught him off guard. Jeez, he outweighed me by a good fifty pounds. If we'd wrestled for another ten seconds, he'd have had me on the ground."

"Okay. But I don't have to like it."

"Do you think I like it? If I didn't live in such a crummy neighborhood, I wouldn't have a gun."

"Why is that?"

"I don't know. Too many strangers, low rents..."

"Not that. Your dad's obviously well off. You've got to be making a decent living."

"Ah." Max's lips curled in a wry smile. "Well, I've made it a point to take care of myself since I got out of college, and the apartment—well, it's a place to sleep."

She studied him for a long moment. "You know, you're not like most of the reporters I've met on Capitol Hill."

"Right. A bunch of TV hacks out to kiss the Senate's butt and pass on their press releases. No, I'm a real newsman. And proud of it."

"So you can't be a real newsman unless you live in a bad neighborhood?"

"Honestly, I hardly consider it. It's just a place to crash. I save my money, go on dates, take vacations. Just like a real person."

"Right. Pizza boxes on tables, laundry on the floor..."

"Hey, when were you in my place?"

"What? I never..." She blushed again as Max laughed out loud.

"Lord. If you'd seen the look on your face."

"So it's true."

"Well, I'm not a very good housekeeper, but there's no pizza boxes. Maybe some Chinese take out..."

"Now I know you're joking."

"You got me. I guess it comes down to the fact that I haven't been with anyone I wanted to impress. What about you? Twenty-eight, still living at home?

She frowned. "It's worked out really well these last few years, what with work and school. But it's temporary. I'm moving soon. Now that I've just got my thesis to write, it should be easier being on my own."

Max nodded, looked as if he was going to say something, but instead, he checked his watch. "Okay. Guess we can get moving."

They got up and put on their coats, Max pocketing the gun, and went to the car. She got in on the passenger side after a brief debate about who would drive. Max was such a guy, he refused to consider her behind the wheel, but if she saw even a hint of tired or woozy, she'd kick him out on his butt.

Although Max was still stiff, he seemed to be making a remarkable recovery. Jade was sure the extra night's sleep had helped.

The winter wonderland out the window captured her attention for a while, but the day they faced wouldn't allow her to enjoy it for too long. "Do you actually have a plan?"

"Sure. Call Peter, call Herb."

"Well that's a hell of a plan, Max. Is that it?"

He smiled at her, then turned his attention back to the narrow road. ''No. I want to find out if Peter interviewed Edith Edwards. Hopefully, he hasn't gone to see her yet. While he's keeping her busy in the living room, we'll go in the back office and take a look at his computer.''

''Isn't that risky?''

''I don't think it's as risky as my talking to her. If Geotech is watching…''

''Do you think they are?''

''At this point, we have to assume they're watching everybody who could help. That's why I haven't called my dad. I don't know what I'd do if something happened to him. Did you see him on the news the other night?''

''He believes in you.''

Max nodded. ''Always has. Even when I've screwed up.''

''Hmm. How have you screwed up?''

''Let me count the ways.''

''Okay.''

He gave her a sharp glance. ''I was joking.''

''I'm not. Come on. Spill.''

Max shook his head as he focused on the drive. Just when she thought he was going to blow off her question, he said, ''I used to drink,'' he said. ''A lot.''

''You don't anymore?''

''Nope. Not really. Although I've slipped a couple of times.''

''Do you go to A.A.?''

''I went to a few meetings. I think the program has a lot of merit, but it's not for me. I'm not the joining type.''

"So how do you do it?"

He shrugged. Winced. "I drank because I was bored. I try not to do that anymore."

"And how do you avoid it?"

He inhaled, let the air go slowly. "I'd like to say that I've developed some fascinating hobbies, but that would be a lie. I work."

"Ah. So you traded one addiction for another?"

"Pretty much."

"And look where it's gotten you."

"There is that."

She shifted in her seat, moving the seat belt to a more comfortable position. "Are you happy?"

He gave her another one of those looks. "What?"

"Happy. You know the concept, I'm sure."

"Hell, I don't know. I don't think about it."

"Think about it now. Are you?"

"I suppose."

"You're willing to risk your life for your work. Don't you think the least you can expect from it is happiness?"

"I believe happiness is an overrated concept. I get satisfaction from doing my job well."

"Satisfaction is good."

He glanced at her. "What about you?"

She stared forward, thinking. "I've been too busy to be happy, but I agree about the reward being a job well done."

"But…?"

She sighed. "I don't have much of a personal life."

"Why not?"

"Work. School."

"Oh, yeah. Tell me about that."

"What's to tell? I'm getting my Ph.D. in poly sci."

"Why?"

"I like it. Actually, I find it fascinating. And it's helped with my job."

"As his assistant."

She nodded. "Which is why I know so much about his life. I do the books, make sure everything is documented. I do his master schedule, although his secretary does most of his correspondence."

"So you don't see it?"

"Not all of it, although every letter out is copied into a master file. He can't blow his nose without some kind of record."

Max quieted as he made the left turn that would take them to town. "That's his public life, not private."

"You think there's a difference? It's not the politics of old, my friend. The game has changed. Everything counts, nothing is free from probing eyes. That's the worst part of it, the fishbowl. Just ask Bill Clinton."

"Don't get me started."

"You wanted to know."

He drove silently for awhile, then slowed the car as he turned to her once more. "Is that it? All you want? To work for your father?"

"No. I want more."

"What, exactly?"

"Boy, you are an investigative reporter."

He grinned, waggled his brows. "Which means you might as well tell me everything because one way or another, I'll find out the truth."

"I could argue with that, but I won't. At least, not right now."

"Good."

"All right. I don't want to run for office. I'm not built that way. I really prefer working with people. I've been thinking a lot lately about teaching."

"You'd be terrific."

"Thank you."

"Just the facts, ma'am."

She sighed, slipped down lower in the comfortable Taurus seat. "I also want a family."

"You'd be terrific at that, too."

She felt her cheeks heat. "Ah, you're just saying that."

"As the man who was nursed by your tender hand, I speak from a position of authority."

"What was I supposed to do? Let you bleed to death?"

"I'm not discussing what you did, but how you did it." His hand touched hers, squeezed gently. "I appreciate it."

She didn't say anything more, just focused on the feel of his cool fingers. Things had gotten a little scary last night, and not because of his wound. Because of her feelings for him. If he hadn't been so weak and so ill, things might have taken a decidedly different turn in bed.

The town came into view, and this time they went to an unfamiliar phone booth.

She decided to do some probing of her own. "What was your father's relationship with Werner Edwards?"

"College buddies. They both went into business

and did well. They ended up living a few blocks apart in Chevy Chase. When I was a kid, he was Uncle Werner.'' Max shook his head, turned away from her.

''You miss him.''

He didn't say anything, just pulled up to the phone booth.

''Peter said you should say you're Frank. He'll change phones and call back.''

Max and Jade got out of the car and crowded into the booth. He dialed, and she leaned closer to listen.

''Peter Shelby.''

''This is Frank.''

''Right. Hey, can I call you back?''

''Sure.'' He read out the number.

''Got it.''

He hung up and they waited, standing so close together he could feel her from shoulder to thigh. He wished they weren't bundled so thickly, that her heat could warm him as it had last night.

He'd awakened just past two to find her body curled around his. Although she'd worn the flannel nightgown, the hem had crawled up to the top of her thighs. Carefully, so as not to wake her, he'd touched her there, run his hand down the length of that warm skin, and gunshot wound be damned, he'd been sorely tempted to turn over, to take her there and then. But he'd held back.

Not that she would have cried foul, he didn't believe that anymore, but because it wasn't right. The two of them were together under the most dire of circumstances. Hell, he'd kidnapped the woman at gunpoint. Her attraction to him might be caused by any number of psychological reasons, none of them having a thing to do with really liking him.

When and if they got together, he wanted it to be because there was something honest between them. On the other hand, if she continued to look at him so enticingly with those big green eyes, he'd act first and ask for forgiveness later.

He jumped when the phone rang, the noise so loud in the quiet of the early morning, he felt as if the whole town had been awakened. "Hello?"

"Frank?"

"Listen, Pete. Have you interviewed Edith Edwards?"

"Not yet. I was gonna talk to Patti."

"Get her later. Can you get to the Edwards's house at—" Max checked his watch "—say, noon?"

"Sure. That's down near your dad's, right?"

"You've got it somewhere, Pete. I'm going to try to get some protection for Patti."

"Any reason you want me there right at noon?"

"It's better for you if you don't know."

"Okay. I guess Jade told you the rest?"

"The account name? Yeah, I got it. You'll be there at noon?"

"You're on. Guess I won't see you there?"

"Not if my luck holds out. Gotta go."

Max hung up and dialed another number. When he connected, he told the operator he was Cho Ming and asked for Herb Bilick. Finally, Herb picked up.

"I was wondering when you'd call."

"Good to talk to you, too, Herb."

"I took your advice and sent some stealth guys to

your apartment. Wow, boy. You were practically media central.''

''What do you mean?''

''Whoever put that stuff there could practically monitor your water usage. Most of it was off-the-shelf crap you can buy in any spy store, but there were a couple of things I've got the lab boys going over even as we speak.''

''Jesus, Herb.''

''What have you got yourself into this time, boy?''

''Deep trouble, is what. Listen, one more thing. You've got to get some protection for Patti Gellar.''

''Patti Gellar?''

''Werner Edwards's secretary.''

''Damn it, Max. How the hell am I supposed to do that without telling my boss what I'm into? I was able to cover up the lab stuff, but this is about manpower. I can't—''

''Go outside the bureau. I mean it, Herb. We were almost killed the other day, and it's not going to stop until Geotech is busted or we're dead. And by we I mean everyone involved.''

Bilick sighed. ''Fine. I'll take care of it. I think I've got something on that guy you asked about. The one with the silver cap?''

''He was the one who tried to kill us. You heard about the shooting at Theodore's in Arlington?''

''Damn, they're not even trying to be subtle. Saw it on the news, but I didn't realize Retik was involved.''

''Retik?''

''Anton Retik. He was in black ops after Vietnam, then turned up as a merc in Africa and South America. Nasty customer. Trained with the Mossad, knew a bunch of ex-NKVD people. He was supposed to have died in Colombia a few years back. Thing is, most people get gold or porcelain caps. He's the only guy in the records with silver."

"Great." Max looked at Jade, inches away. "I'll get back to you."

"Sure you wouldn't like to turn yourself in?"

Max hung up.

"Well?" Jade looked at him.

"I was luckier than I thought with Silver Tooth. He's a stone killer. A total professional."

"Oh, that makes me feel so much better." She inched out of the phone booth. "What about Peter?"

"He's going to talk to Edith Edwards. As for us, we're on our way to new careers as cat burglars."

"Oh boy."

They got back in the car, and put on seat belts. "We've got an hour before we have to be on the road. Any ideas?"

"Why don't we get where we're going early and check it out. Make sure there are no surprises."

Max grinned. "You sure you've never done any of this cloak-and-dagger stuff before?"

"Nope. Never."

"Well, honey, you're good."

After they got back on the road, he hit the highway toward Chevy Chase, Maryland.

Traffic was snarled, so they didn't have as much time as he'd hoped when they turned down Nevada Avenue. Jade was struck by the festive look of the street. Trees and houses were strung with lights, and the snow gave everything a fairyland quality. "Nice neighborhood."

"Yeah. They really go all out at Christmas. That's the house where I grew up."

Jade studied the two-story brick house. She imagined the elder Mr. Travis sitting alone in the large home with the colorful lights dark, hoping his son would soon be safe. It wasn't a big leap to think of her own father, waiting, worrying. "Max?"

"Yeah?"

He spoke distractedly as he cased the streets, driving a few miles under the speed limit.

"I need to let my father know I'm all right."

He turned sharply toward her. "Are you crazy?"

"No. I'm not," she said, sitting up straighter in her seat. "I know he's out of his mind with worry. I can't do that to him."

"We've talked about this. You have to. If you think Geotech was monitoring me, can you imagine what they're doing to your father?"

"So what? They already know we're together. As long as we pick some out of the way phone booth, what difference would it make?"

He stopped the car. Looked at her for a long moment. "Let me think this through, okay?"

She was going to argue with him, but she held back. His life was at stake. So was hers. It wasn't a bad idea to consider her proposal. She didn't want anyone to get hurt. "Fine. But I'm not going to let it drop. I should have done this days ago."

"We have to be careful. More careful than we've ever been in our lives."

"I understand."

When they were on Oakland Road, Max pulled over behind another car and parked. ''That's Werner's house,'' he said, pointing.

''Why park here?''

''A lone car is more likely to be noticed than a pair.'' He turned the engine off. ''Peter should be along soon.''

They sat quietly. Jade noticed pops and crackles as the engine cooled down. The occasional dog barked. She rolled the window down and was startled at the coldness of the gentle breeze.

She turned to Max, puzzled. ''If Geotech is so swell at covering all the bases, what makes you think Werner's computer wasn't stolen?''

Max shrugged. ''We won't know until we get in. I will say that he told me he was very careful never to leave any computer evidence at Geotech. And I think we would have heard about a break-in at the house. The papers would have been all over that.''

At the sound of a vehicle approaching from behind, Max scrunched down in the seat, motioning for her to do the same. Peeking over the dashboard, they saw a black Cadillac pass and drive to the next corner, then turn right.

They remained in position. Jade's heart pumped so hard she thought surely Max could hear it, but a glance at him found him staring intently at the rearview mirror. She closed her eyes and breathed deeply, willing herself to relax.

''There's Peter. Guess he liked his car so much he rented one just like it.''

Jade opened her eyes to see a silver-gray Taurus pull to the curb several houses ahead. Wearing what looked like a cashmere coat, Peter got out. ''Are you going to let him know we're here?''

Max shook his head. ''No. We'll wait till he's inside, then go around back.''

Her heart pounded harder, which she hadn't thought was possible.

Peter walked to the front door and rang the doorbell. As he waited, he stamped his feet and looked up and down the block, but showed no sign of having seen his own car, or the passengers inside.

A minute later, a short, white-haired woman answered the door. She and Peter exchanged words, then disappeared inside.

''Maid?'' Jade asked.

Max shook his head. ''For all their money, they're just plain folks. When I was a kid, Edith would bake pies or cakes or something every time we visited. That's why I'm pretty confident about sneaking in. I know that place as well as my own. Let's hit it.''

Jade scrambled to catch up with Max, pulling her baseball cap more firmly down on her head. Max headed back as though he belonged.

The yards were marginally separated with three to four foot high boxwood hedgerows, and Max suddenly darted down the one on the far side of the Edwards's house, Jade on his heels. After they were past the edge of the house, Max stopped and waited for her. ''They'll be in the parlor on the other side of the house,'' he whispered.

''You know that?''

''I know Edith Edwards, and I know this house. C'mon.'' He walked toward the back.

There was a large hedge separating the side yard

from the back, and Max bent to the right, pulling a large branch aside, exposing a hole in the fence behind. ''You first.''

Jade bent and crawled through the exposed hole, closely followed by Max.

When they were both standing in the backyard, they brushed the snow from their hands and knees.

''We're going to have to go through the kitchen,'' Max whispered. ''Peter and Edith will be at the front of the house, down the hall. We're going to go in and across the hall on the right.''

She nodded. ''How do we get in?''

Max grinned like a small boy and pulled out a Swiss Army knife. ''I never missed MacGyver.'' He moved to the back door then inserted the blade between the door frame and the screen door.

Moments later, there was a sharp click as the latch opened. ''They never did lock the inside door.'' He put his hand on the knob and turned.

The door opened. With a finger to his lips, Max stepped in and held the door for her.

Jade followed him, holding her hand out to prevent the screen door from slamming. She found it difficult to breathe, she was so nervous. The excitement of the cloak-and-dagger business was highly overrated.

As Max carefully closed the door, they heard muffled voices down the central hall. Max jerked his head sideways and headed for the side door to another hallway. A board squeaked and he stopped, hand held up in warning. The quiet hum of distant voices never stopped. Max moved on.

They went up six steps across a small landing with stairs going up to the second floor on the left, then down six steps on the other side. The place was gorgeous, decorated with such attention to detail she would have liked to take her time, look at every nook and cranny.

The walls, painted a deep red with the most beautiful crown molding she'd ever seen, were the perfect complement to the cream and beige chaise, which had been artfully draped with a cashmere throw. Caught up in her surroundings, she walked into Max as he stopped in front of a pair of closed sliding doors.

Ignoring her blunder, Max slipped his fingers into the brass notches and pushed sideways.

Nothing. He looked at Jade worriedly and pushed again, harder. With what seemed like a deafening squeak, the doors lurched sideways about a foot. They both stood stock still, not breathing.

There was no cry of alarm, no hurried footsteps. After long seconds, Jade let her breath out with a whoosh. Max pushed the doors a few inches farther apart and edged in sideways, and she followed. He pulled the doors closed more easily. ''Probably stuck,'' he whispered.

Jade nodded and giggled, evoking a peculiar look from him. Never in her life had she envisioned herself doing this kind of thing. Despite her terror, she had to admit it excited her immensely. There was definitely the element of danger, yet at the same time, she felt relatively safe with Max. After all, he knew the house and the woman who lived in it. What was the worst that could happen? Then she remembered Retik, and the exhilaration turned back into fear.

She followed Max to the desk, and he sat in the

well-worn leather-covered chair and hit the computer's on switch.

It was quiet, except for the sound of their breathing, and the whines and clicks of the computer, and Jade had the opportunity to take in her surroundings.

She was in a relatively large room, paneled in a richly stained mahogany, with matching bookshelves, many with glass doors. The desk, with a pair of overstuffed occasional chairs, sat comfortably near a window that looked out onto the expansive backyard, and all these pieces rested on an ancient Persian rug that had obviously been treated with a lot of care and respect.

"Aha," Max said, and she looked over his shoulder to see the computer was ready. With a combination of the mouse and keyboard, Max began searching through the files. He clicked on a folder named "Geotech," and a window opened.

It required a password.

"Damn," Max whispered.

"Any ideas?"

"Lots, but we need to get out of here before Peter's done." He opened a couple of the desk drawers, finally finding a box of new floppy disks. He pulled a couple out, put one in the drive of the computer, and copied the entire folder to floppy. It all fit on one, and Max removed it, then repeated the process with the other. "Better have two. Sometimes these things self-destruct if you get the wrong password."

Jade nodded, and Max handed her the first floppy as the second copied. She stuck it in her coat pocket.

When the second copy finished, Max removed it

from the computer and bent to turn it off. Jade heard the sound of the sliding doors opening and looked over with her heart in her mouth to see a pair of long-lashed blue eyes looking straight into her own.

Chapter Nine

"Hello. Are you a friend of Grammy's?" It was a boy, dark haired, dressed in a denim jumper with a red plaid shirt underneath. He looked to be about four or five.

"Hi, Adam. It's Uncle Max. Remember me?" Max stepped from behind the desk and put a protective arm around Jade. He smiled at the boy, but kept his voice low.

Adam stared back at him for a long time, then his gaze moved to Jade. "What are you doing?"

"We're playing hide-and-seek. What are you doing?"

"It's nap time, but I wasn't sleepy."

Max released Jade and walked, slightly bent over, to the boy. He put a hand on his slender shoulder. "You want to play with us?"

The little face broke into a broad grin, lacking one of his front teeth. "Okay."

"All righty, then. Since you're getting in the game late, you're going to have to be 'it.'"

The child's face fell. Max glanced at Jade with a

forced smile. ''Okay, you don't have to be 'it.' I'll be 'it.'''

The boy's grin returned and he practically hopped from foot to foot in excitement. ''Okay. I can hide good. Real good.''

''Okay, Adam. But we've got to be real quiet, okay? Grammy's got visitors, and we don't want to disturb anybody.''

''Okay.''

''Now, I'm going to hide my eyes, count to a hundred, and you two go hide.''

Jade looked at him, one eyebrow raised.

''Kitchen,'' Max whispered.

She nodded, and Max went to the desk and bent over the computer monitor with his head on his arm. ''One, two, three...''

Adam scampered off down the hall. Jade touched Max on the shoulder. ''He's gone,'' she whispered.

''Let's get out of here.'' Max grabbed her arm and whisked her out of Werner's library, closing the doors as quietly as he could, and hurried her back toward the kitchen.

They could still hear Edith and Peter in the parlor, and Max opened the back door and screen and motioned Jade through.

Once in the backyard, he hurried for the hole in the fence, going through first and holding the branch for her, then practically ran down the hedgerow, only slowing as they reached the sidewalk.

''Oh, my God. Who the hell was that? I thought my heart was going to pop out of my chest.''

''Yeah. Surprise.'' Max smiled grimly. ''That was Werner's grandson.''

"If you know him, how come we rushed?"

"He can only count to thirty. If he gets bored and goes looking for us, it would be better if the whole thing gets chalked up to his imagination."

"But he knows you."

Max nodded, wincing. "True. I don't believe Edith thinks I killed Werner. She knows me too well. But I don't want to put her in danger. Maybe Adam will say something in front of Peter. He'll do the damage control. But dammit, the last thing I want is for Geotech to think there's something worth finding at the house."

They walked to the car, Max moving slowly, holding his side. After they got in, he sat for a moment, then turned to her. "You have any aspirin in that purse of yours?"

She nodded, then went into the zipper pouch where she had a small tin of extra-strength aspirin. Max didn't even bother to wait for a drink, he just swallowed three pills.

"Now what?" Jade asked, as Max started the car and headed back to town.

Max's frown deepened. "I'm not sure. I guessed he would use passwords, but I didn't think to bring the laptop."

"What about the Gellar woman? Would she know the password?"

"If anybody did. But her phone number is on the laptop, too. We need to get back to the cabin," he said. Max suddenly pulled to the curb and rested his head on his hands. "You're going to have to drive."

Jade could see the pain in his face, the slim lines around his eyes, the way his lips pressed together so hard they were pale white. In the excitement of her first—and hopefully last—housebreaking, it had been easy to forget that Max had been shot a mere two days ago. Despite her disappointment that they'd done the two-hour drive for so little, she gently placed her hand on his shoulder.

"Are you bleeding?"

He shook his head. "I don't think so. Just hurting. And incredibly tired." The sound of his door opening surprised her, as did the cold wash of wind that flew into her face. Max stumbled, but caught himself on the fender as they passed. She wanted to help him, but she could do that best by driving him home.

Once reseated and belted in, he leaned his head against the seat back and closed his eyes.

Jade drove back toward the freeway, worried about Max, about the password, even about Peter. As she exited the crowded population center of the D.C. area, she remembered they were almost out of gauze. He'd said he wasn't bleeding, but she didn't know if it was true, or if it would last. They also needed more topical antiseptic and more pain medication. It shouldn't be too dangerous to hit a small town drugstore. No one would think to look for them, and if Max stayed in the car, she could dash in and out without raising an alarm.

Another glance at Max told her he was asleep. His mouth had opened slightly, but his breathing seemed steady and regular. She couldn't see his wound through his coat. The risk was worth it, she needed to get the supplies.

The decision made, she began looking for an exit that would take her down a small-town main street.

Someplace she'd never heard of, that wasn't directly off the highway.

She pulled off, stopped at the bottom of the off-ramp, and then turned right. A sign at the corner mentioned a town five miles east. She headed for it, past gas stations, convenience marts and auto shops. Finally, she saw the sign for Main Street, and she turned there.

She spotted a drugstore down the street and pulled into a parking place.

Max still slept. She thought about leaving him a note, but she'd be back so fast, it really wouldn't matter.

After settling her baseball cap on her head, she went into the drugstore. It wasn't like the chain drugstore near her home, cheerless and sterile. There she'd never considered wandering the aisles. Here, the shelves were close together and stuffed with goodies. It was hard not to slow down and browse.

As she looked for gauze she caught a movement from the corner of her eye.

A large man, dressed in denims and heavy shoes, wearing a heavy, brightly checked coat and a hunting cap with the earflaps tied on top. He glanced at her face and looked away quickly.

Jade's stomach churned with a jolt of paranoia. She told herself she was imagining things. He was probably a harmless pervert. Nothing to get upset about. But why had he looked away so quickly? Dammit, he'd recognized her. Which wasn't part of the plan.

She moved down the aisle. The pharmacist's booth was at the back, and that's where she was going to find the supplies she really needed. She looked around just in time to see the man in the checked coat step into her aisle, looking toward her.

Okay. Should she bolt or buy the supplies? Mostly she wanted to run, but if she did, wouldn't that look terribly suspicious? Dammit, she wasn't good at this stuff. She'd thought she'd been scared when they were breaking and entering, but this being on the lam thing totally sucked.

Okay, so no bolting. Buying is what she'd do. Casual. Like Jane Normal, nothing suspicious about her, no sir. She moved purposefully down the aisle and found the gauze on a lower shelf. As she stood, she found herself exactly opposite the checked-coat man, and his eyes widened in recognition.

She turned her face away, looking desperately for the adhesive tape, cursing her decision not to bolt. Now it was too late, and he really did recognize her, and instead of being on the street, she was stuck in the store. At least she wasn't with Max, that was something. But if the cops came, they'd find him, wounded and asleep in Peter's car, and that wasn't good.

Just as she was about to hide the gauze in with the condoms, she saw checked-coat exit the front door and hurry away to the right.

She stopped at the cashier. Her gaze caught on a display of hair dye, and she picked up two boxes, both blonde. Then she gave the woman a twenty-dollar bill, got the change and headed for the front door.

As she left the store, she glanced to her right and saw checked-coat talking excitedly to another man, similarly dressed, except in a plain brown coat not unlike her own. Before she could turn away, checked-coat pointed at her, and the two men started down the sidewalk toward her.

She turned left, walking toward the car. But if she got in, they'd have the license plate. She passed it, walking rapidly. She could see Max was still slumped back asleep.

Quickened footsteps closed in behind her. She looked at the upcoming shops frantically. There, a coffee shop.

When she walked in, a little bell rang over the door.

The shop could only be described as "quaint." There were ten or twelve small round tables scattered about, all with cloth tablecloths. Four people were sitting at three of the tables, and there was a glass showcase at the back with a selection of pastries. Jade looked back and saw the two men hesitate outside.

She used the moment to rush to the back of the coffee shop, to the bathroom. As she'd hoped, there was a door leading to the alley. There was a sign on it; Do Not Open This Door Except in Case of Emergency. This qualified, but she prayed it wasn't connected to an alarm.

A quick survey of the alley showed her nothing but garbage cans next to the wall near the door, so she took a deep breath and pushed the door open and stepped out, wincing as she listened for bells and whistles. Nothing.

She was so scared she was practically hyperventilating, and that wouldn't do. She stepped away from the door and paused in another doorway.

When she got her breath, she peeked out, looking both ways. Trash and garbage cans lined the alley, but no people were in sight. She stepped out and walked rapidly toward the street, avoiding puddles and bits of trash when she could.

Okay, so she'd been made. She hadn't really kept up with the news, but she wouldn't be surprised if her father had posted a reward for her, which made her visit to Mayberry very stupid indeed. Still, those men didn't look very slick.

The problem was how to get them away from the car. If they saw the car, there would be no safe haven for her and Max. God, Max.

After taking a deep breath, she walked along the sidewalk to the edge of the buildings and stopped, then peeked around the corner, trying to keep from attracting the attention of the townsfolk.

The men were still outside the coffee shop, looking away from her.

Jade stepped out around the corner. If they turned toward her, she'd run back to the alley. Otherwise…

As quickly as she could, she slipped inside a shop that sold coats and luggage.

The room was redolent with the odor of leather, kind of like a giant new car. There were racks of coats and shelves of suitcases, trunks, and purses. Displays of matched luggage poked into the aisles. Christmas music played over the speakers. She moved deeper into the store, trying not to panic. She took her coat off and put it across her arm, then started looking at the racks in earnest.

She saw a three-quarter length wool coat that wasn't too bad. She tossed her own coat across the rail and picked up the wool one, then went to one of the full-length mirrors.

Nervous hysteria surged in her chest and she actually laughed at herself. The image of her standing there with the baseball cap and the coat. She took the cap off and shook her hair out.

Not bad. She could probably get away with the pants and shoes. Men might check out a woman's legs, but they'd never look at her shoes. She went to the counter at the back.

The teenage salesgirl behind the counter was reading a book and blowing on her nails, almost dropping the book when Jade looked over the counter. "Oh, sorry. Can I help you?" She tried to put the book down and stand without using her fingers.

"I'd like to buy this coat. I'll wear it out. And can you put this stuff in a bag?" She handed the salesgirl her short coat, baseball cap, and bag from the drugstore. "Do you have a bathroom?"

"Sure. Over there." The girl waved her hand to a door to the side.

Jade smiled and nodded. "I'll be right back to pay for it."

Once in the bathroom, she combed her hair and put on lipstick. She looked at herself while turning her head side to side and decided it would have to do.

Back at the counter, the girl had managed to get her nails dry enough to take care of business, for the coat had the tags removed and was lying across the counter. Everything else was in a large plastic bag with the store's name on it.

"Sunglasses?" Jade asked.

"Sure." The girl led her to a rack in the corner.

Jade grabbed a pair that would cover a lot of her face, then went back to the counter. She paid for everything, then put on the coat and sunglasses, picked up the bag, and strode out of the store like she owned the town.

As she walked down the sidewalk, glancing in the windows, the second man came running from the café. The two talked rapidly, then split up, running to the opposite ends of the street, checked-coat going right past Jade.

She grinned but walked damn fast to the car. Max was still asleep. She tossed her bag into the back seat, buckled up and got the hell out of Dodge.

Max slept all the way to the little town near the cabin. She went right to the department store where she'd bought his robe, and left him in the car. This time, she made sure not to make eye contact with anyone as she hurried through the store. She bought six big towels, a hair dryer, a set of sheets and a couple of pairs of boxers for Max. No one looked her way, and she avoided the gaze of the cashier. By the time she made it back to the car, she was as jumpy as a cat, and all she wanted was to be home.

Max shifted, turning his head to the left when she started the car, but he didn't wake up until she parked in the garage.

It took him a minute to gather his senses, but by the time they were inside, he seemed more chipper. He stopped, in fact, in the middle of taking off his jacket. "Whoa. New coat, nice do. What did I miss?" He ran his hand through his hair and rubbed his eyes.

"I wanted to get some more medical supplies and some guys spotted me. Come on, let's get you into bed."

"Excuse me?"

She took off her new purchase and hung it up on

the rack. ''I stopped in a little town and got some gauze. We're just about out.''

''Fast forward to the guys who spotted you, please?''

''They saw me, but I ditched them.''

''Ditched them?''

''Yep. Just like James Bond. Without Q, of course. It was actually pretty cool.'' She went to the kitchen to brew up a pot of coffee. ''I lost them by going through a coffee shop, then into another store where I bought that coat and sunglasses. It was exciting.''

''Exciting.'' Max sat down at the small table. ''What was your take on them? Were these guys professionals or—''

''No, no. I'd stopped at a small town. They were locals. I figure my dad must have offered a reward.''

''Yeah. I guess.'' He seemed a little relieved, but not convinced.

She didn't speak while counting out the coffee grounds. ''They didn't see the car. Or you.''

''But you can be sure they'll call the police.''

''I know,'' she said, pressing the on button. She sat down across from him and ran a hand through her hair, liking the feel of it down. ''But they still won't find us. Because I also got us disguises.''

''Funny noses? Dark glasses?''

''Nope. Hair dye. They say blondes have more fun.''

''Blondes?''

''Everyone's on the lookout for us dark-haired types. I figured it would help.''

''It's a good idea. But blonde?''

"You'll be devastatingly handsome. Women will have to be held back by force."

"Ah, so nothing will change, eh?"

She grinned. "You wish. But listen, the whole reason I stopped was to get you new bandages. So why don't we take a look at that side of yours."

He winced, although she figured it was just the idea of changing the dressing, and not from actual pain. "Right."

She went to her coat and got the drugstore goodies and the floppy disk out of the plastic bag. That, she put on the table, next to the laptop.

Max reached for it, but she stopped him with her hand on his arm. "After."

He frowned. Then started unbuttoning his shirt. "I wish to hell I could figure out the password. I know there's enough evidence on that floppy to hang Geotech."

While she filled a small bowl with hot water, it occurred to her that he'd said Geotech, and not her father. Had he reconsidered? Doubtful. He was just being polite. Despite the change in the dynamic, what with her hiding him, abetting him, and all, he still figured her father was a player in this far too dangerous game.

She'd just have to prove him wrong, that's all. Prove that whatever her father's faults, he was honest, decent.

Perhaps the files would be just the evidence she'd need. They had to figure out that password.

But first, Max. She removed the old gauze and was grateful to see that despite it being pretty gross, he hadn't bled much. There was a discharge, but it didn't smell rank, so she figured there wasn't an infection, which was damn lucky. With much steadier fingers than when she'd first doctored him, she bathed the wound, smeared it with antiseptic, then taped it up again. She made Max put the stuff away while she booted the laptop.

When she tried to open the folder, she got the same thing Max had at the house: password required.

Knowing nothing about Werner Edwards, she searched the hard drive for "Edwards," and then "Werner," writing down any peripheral names she came across. Although she was certainly no hacker, having been largely in a position where she simply called tech support whenever there was a computer problem, she did know that most people used common names and dates familiar to them when setting passwords—spouses, children, grandchildren, birthdays.

There hadn't been any dates on Max's computer relative to Werner, but she found his daughter's name, and she tried that first. Cecelia.

Nope. She tried Edith. Nope. Adam. Nope. In frustration, she ejected the floppy and turned the laptop off. This was why Max had talked about getting in touch with Patti Gellar.

Jade sighed.

"No luck, I take it." Max, sitting across from her, looked sleepy again. She imagined all this tiredness was his body's reaction to the healing process. The more he slept, the faster he'd heal. But first, he needed something to eat.

"Not yet." She got up and made him a quick ham and cheese sandwich, remembering that he liked lettuce, but not tomato. She also heated up some more soup.

He was actually asleep sitting up when she brought him his food. ''I'm not—''

''Eat,'' she said. ''You have to get better, so just consider it medicine.''

''Yes, ma'am.''

She smiled as she sat down across from him. Not terribly hungry herself, she'd decided just to have soup, so they shared the meal quietly. Jade found herself watching him eat, watching his long fingers, the sparse, masculine hair on the back of his hands. His jaw muscle worked as he ate, and his brows, thick but not messy, bowed in concentration. When her gaze moved to his eyes, she was struck again by the color, the blue clear and lighter than one would have expected given his dark hair.

With a shock, she realized he was staring right back at her, curiosity evident in the arch of his right brow.

She flushed, looked away, embarrassed that he'd caught her.

''What were you thinking?'' he asked.

''What?''

He chuckled as he put the last of his sandwich on his plate. ''We've been through too much to get shy now. You had the most interesting expression on your face. I couldn't help but wonder—''

''Fine,'' she said, busying herself with her cup. ''I was thinking that your eyes are much bluer than I would have imagined.''

''Ah. Black Irish.''

She cocked her head. ''Travis?''

"Father's side. My mother's maiden name was O'Brien."

"I see."

"What about you?"

"I don't know."

His lips pressed together. "I'm sorry. I forgot."

"Not a problem. I was abandoned as an infant. It was quite prosaic, actually. Left on the steps of a church."

"That must have been hard for you."

"Only in my teenage years, when I was so desperate to find myself. My parents tried their best to find out about my past, but it was no good. I saw a TV program years ago where an adopted girl had some incurable illness that only her real parents could cure, and that had me obsessed for months. I was sure I would die a very dramatic death. You know, one of those film deaths where my major symptom would be getting more and more beautiful as my demise approached."

He laughed. "Yeah, I've seen that. Tragic."

"Right. But I've had all sorts of medical tests and I'm ridiculously healthy. Whoever my parents were, they didn't carry an inherited disorder. Except perhaps Alzheimer's, but I won't know about that for a few years."

"What was it like, being adopted?"

"Great. Scary at first, just because I had no idea who my new parents were. But I got over that quickly. I was lucky, extraordinarily so. I had a great childhood."

"I'll bet."

"You still don't believe me, about my father, I

know that. But by the time this is resolved, you'll see.''

He reached over and touched the back of her hand. ''I hope so.''

Her cheeks heated again, for a different reason this time. His touch made things happen inside her. The reaction wasn't a shock, but the strength of it was. Somewhere between the kidnapping and her daring escape this afternoon, she'd become deeply attracted to this man. This fugitive.

''You know, you had a prime opportunity this afternoon. To go back to your life.''

''I also had one two days ago, if you remember.''

''Yeah.'' He shook his head, his expression bewildered. ''You could have gone home. They'd have protected you.''

''I know that, too.''

''So why didn't you?''

She turned her hand over, threaded her fingers through his. ''I want to help.''

''Why?''

''I was almost killed, too, you know.''

''That's not it. At least, I don't think so.''

''You mean you think I stayed because of you.''

His gaze caught hers once more, and this time there was something much more complex than curiosity there. ''Yeah. That's what I think.''

She knew she was blushing, that she should have taken back her hand, looked away, denied it, but since she was living smack dab in the middle of bizzaro world, she looked right back at him. ''You're right. I'm here because of you. I believe you. In you.''

"That's not the smartest move, you know. Lots and lots of people think I'm a crackpot. A killer."

She smiled. "Ah, they're just uninformed. About the killer part at least. The jury's still out about you being a nut."

He smiled in return. Didn't say anything, kept her gaze locked on his. Ran his thumb lightly over her hand. And then he leaned over the cups and the salt shaker and touched her lips with his own.

It wasn't a movie kiss, but it packed a wallop nonetheless. Soft, tender, lips on lips, gentle breath. Then it deepened ever so slightly and his tongue brushed the crease. She opened her mouth and let him taste her. As nice as that was, she needed more. To taste him right back.

And then it was a movie kiss because he stood up, pulled her up with him, never breaking the contact between them, and she was in his arms instead of just holding his hand, and there was heat wherever they touched, especially in the kiss, in the way he explored her, teased her. Their tongues slid together in hot, electric contact, making her reaction to his caress of her hand seem like the minor leagues.

He ran a hand down her back, pulling her closer, stroking her through her sweater. She could feel that she wasn't the only one who was having a strong reaction. His erection pressed against her hip, hard and insistent.

He moved his mouth to the corner of her lips, kissing her lightly, then sliding down to her neck where he found the sensitive flesh below her ear.

She moaned as her head lolled back. A stray thought, unwelcome in this state of bliss, told her she was enjoying this so much because it was forbidden, dangerous. Because it was bizzaro world and none of the rules applied.

And then she didn't care. Not a whit. Because he'd come back up to find her lips. With a daring she barely recognized, she thrust her tongue in his mouth. Instantly rewarded with a deep, guttural moan, she grew bolder still, moving her hand between them, slightly below his chest. Then lower.

Chapter Ten

Pain was a distant memory as Max responded to Jade's touch. Her hand, small, delicate, ran down the front of his jeans, moving slower by the inch. Her kiss, on the other hand, had become increasingly urgent, and the combination was nothing short of combustible.

He wanted her closer although he had to be careful not to pull her too close to his injury, because he'd rather bleed to death than stop.

She smelled so damn good. Like winter and spring mixed together, like heaven and earth, and he couldn't get enough. That didn't even come close to the way she felt. The curve of her hip, the softness teasing him beneath her sweater… Too many clothes, not enough skin.

He slipped his right hand underneath her sweater and she gasped. The surprise for him came a second later when she breathed again, her soft sweetness slipping between his lips.

"Jade," he whispered.

"I know," she said, then turned her head to the left before she kissed him again.

Her hand had reached his erection, and he cursed the denim while he thanked the powers that be for giving him this moment, this woman. She wasn't tentative, which if he'd given it any thought, would have surprised him, but he wasn't capable of such complex views. Not while she traced his length with the palm of her hand, making him impossibly harder.

Her palm disappeared, as did her lips. He opened his eyes, ready to beg if he had to, to see her frowning. "What's wrong?"

"I'm molesting a wounded man."

"I'm fine," he said. "Really."

She stepped back, and he bit back a moan. "Two minutes ago you said you were exhausted. That you needed to sleep."

"I was insane."

She smiled, but she didn't come back. "No. It's really dumb, Max. You need to get well. Too much depends on you being on your toes."

"I promise, I'll be careful."

"You say that now..."

He looked down between them. "You do realize in many states this is considered cruel and unusual punishment."

She frowned prettily. "Yeah, I think I heard that line when I was fourteen. It hasn't become more credible over time, however."

"You're a hard woman, Jade Parker."

She looked between them, too. "Nope, I think that title belongs to you."

"My point, exactly."

"Go shower. Now's a perfect time to use that hair dye. When you're finished, I'll do the same. I'm going to clean up here, then try to figure out Werner's password.''

He looked at her, trying to figure out if he could change her mind, but she seemed determined. With a kiss, as teasing as he could make it, he left her standing in the middle of the small cabin, so that he could take care of himself in the shower. But first, he picked up the box of Lady Clairol and read the back. ''So I just put this gunk on and let it sit?''

''Yep. We'll both probably need to let it develop for a long time, seeing as how we have such dark hair.''

He narrowed his eyes. ''Are you sure about this?''

''We're sitting targets, Max. Let's at least try to give ourselves a break.''

He nodded, then took his box, along with a couple of towels, into the bathroom.

Jade stood quite still while he closed the door. Then she collapsed in the wooden chair. ''Holy…'' She put her head down on her arm, trying hard to slow her heart rate, telling her libido to shut the hell up. It wasn't easy.

She hadn't felt like that for…well, ever. Not ever. She'd been a wild woman, ready to throw him on the bed and ravish him.

It must be all this spy stuff. Living on the edge. Being a fugitive agreed with her, evidently. If the stakes weren't so very, very high, she'd really enjoy herself, but she'd been right to put the brakes on. If she'd re-opened his wound, they'd be in deep trouble. He had to be well, alert, agile, to get through this and she had to be on her toes, as well. This afternoon had shown her that.

With a deep breath, she got up, cleared the dishes. The water flowed in the bathroom, so she held off washing the dishes. She didn't want him to get a sudden spray of cold. If he wanted that, he'd have to do it himself.

So she went back to the laptop. She kept trying different combinations of names, dates, anything she could think of, but it was no use.

"Any luck?"

Jade jumped. She hadn't heard the bathroom door open. When she turned, it took her a moment to adjust to the new, maybe not so improved Max. He was blonde, all right. Not Britney Spears blonde, but close. It looked…weird.

"What do you think?" he asked.

"You don't look like you."

"That's good, right?"

"Yep."

He scowled. "I'm hideous. You want to run screaming out into the snow."

"No, no. Not at all. It just takes some getting used to."

"Well, don't be too smug. You're next." He walked up to her, put his hand on her shoulder. "So, nothing, huh?"

"Not a lick."

He didn't say anything, just gave her a reassuring squeeze.

"How are you?"

"A little tired."

"See, I told you."

"Not that tired."

"Go to bed. I've got to do the whole hair thing,

and mine won't be as quick. We should probably catch the news, too."

He grunted, but then he kissed the back of her neck. The goosebumps covered her whole body, and when she went to log off the computer, her hands trembled.

This was one tiny cabin to contain all this sexual tension. Maybe a cold shower wasn't a bad idea.

SHE TURNED OFF the hair dryer and looked at herself in the bathroom mirror. The lighter hair wasn't as bad as she'd feared, but she hadn't turned into Marilyn Monroe, either. Maybe after she got used to it, she'd like it better. The important thing was that she didn't look like herself. A stranger would have to be perceptive to realize that she was the kidnapped woman on the news.

Jade turned the lights out, then looked over at Max to make sure he was really asleep. He didn't move, so she slipped her clothes off and climbed into bed.

She was tired, and the wise thing would be to curl up into her own little ball and go directly to sleep. But being so close to his warmth tempted her beyond her ability to be good, and she shifted until the front of her body pressed against his back.

It wasn't enough. She snuggled closer, pressing her breasts against his back and putting her arm over his body with her hand on his chest.

A little moan escaped from his throat, but it wasn't from pain. Experimentally, she moved her hand, feeling his pectorals, running her fingers through the thin hair on his chest.

"Jade?" He stirred, rolling onto his back.

"Shhh." She put a gentle index finger to his lips. "Go back to sleep."

He didn't say anything for a long time, time enough for her to make peace with the fact that he'd done just as she'd asked him.

"Screw this," he whispered, and before she could utter a false protest his lips were on hers.

She needed no further encouragement, picking things up right where they'd left off. Kissing him lit her up inside, and her hand went right to the buttons of his pajamas, not at all pleased that he wasn't as naked as she.

His hand joined hers in undoing his buttons. Since he seemed to have that covered, she moved down to undo the tie at his waist, anxious to get his bottoms off as quickly as possible.

They parted, briefly, while he pushed his bottoms off and kicked them away. Both of them got his top off, and soon it was on the floor, too.

Naked, shivering, they curled up together under the covers. His hand moved across her stomach, causing ripples of sensation to run along the length of her body as he bent over her to capture her in another kiss. She sighed and lifted her hand to pull his lips tighter to her own as her stomach muscles twitched uncontrollably.

He cupped her breast and she gasped at the touch, so soft, with a sense of restrained strength. She arched her back to fill his hand and felt the heat stir between her legs.

His lips slipped to her neck while his hand caressed her breast, his fingers brushing her nipple. It responded immediately as though it had a will of its own, stiffening to a hard little button.

With his lips, he brushed the curve where her neck met her shoulders, and she moaned. She stretched her hand to touch his chest, then slid her palm down to his solid stomach. He shivered with pleasure and pressed against her, and she could feel the hardness of him against her thigh. His fingers returned to her nipple and she moaned again, involuntarily turning her head back and forth as his fingers toyed with her nipples until they were like little diamonds capping her breasts.

She slid her hand lower on his body as his lips took the place of his fingers, and his hardness filled her palm. She arched her back, her legs spreading as the heat built in her belly. She felt her own moisture building.

He rolled onto her and she welcomed the masculine weight of him.

He slid down, kissing her breasts where they met her chest, then moving to her stomach. She locked her fingers in his hair and thrust her hips against his chest, a series of cries echoing in the cabin, cries from her own throat.

His hands parted her legs and his lips tortured her, kissing first one thigh, then the other, ever closer to the center of her torment until finally his tongue flicked across the hard little nub, first slowly, then faster, then faster still.

She responded to the rhythm of his tongue by moving against him, up and down, as the feeling built in her until it washed up through her body from her toes to the top of her head, then back again, and she collapsed to the sheets, spent.

But Max wasn't finished yet. The lips that had just brought her to ecstasy moved back across her stomach to her breast, and she felt the tip of hardness on her thigh.

"Wait," she whispered.

"What's wrong?"

She reached over the side of the bed to the box of condoms she'd bought. Grabbing one, she handed it to him. It was difficult to be patient while he prepared, but finally, he was back.

She reached down to guide him into her, and was rewarded with his moan.

It was slow, too slow, and she thrust her hips so he would fill her faster, but he pulled back, making his entrance into her a sensory experience.

She gasped.

His only response was the continuing controlled pressure as he thrust slowly deeper and deeper into her, until she thought she was full, yet there was more.

"Oh, God." Still, Max continued pushing until she was fuller than she'd ever thought possible, his body pressed tightly to hers. Nearly as slowly, he began to withdraw and she mewed and tried to slide her body against his, but his arms, suddenly so strong, held her. He withdrew then thrust again, this time slightly faster.

She relaxed into his rhythm, her tender parts feeling every glide of skin over skin. Gradually, his speed increased. The sensation built in her toes again, and she put her hands on his buttocks and pulled him against her, again and again, their breath mixing in the cold air, faster and faster, until the shudders washed through them both, and Max collapsed on her with a groan, gasping for breath.

"Are you okay?" she asked.

He kissed her then, gently. "You have to ask?"

"I meant your wound."

"Oh, that. Yeah. Fine. Never better."

She poked him in the arm. "I'm serious."

"Nothing bad happened. I promise."

"Okay."

"Are you a blonde?"

"Yes."

"Can I see?"

"Tomorrow."

He moved to kiss her again, but she stopped him. "Just this once, you have my permission to roll over and go to sleep."

"What if I don't want to?"

"Tough."

"Boy, one day of breaking—"

"Don't forget entering."

His chuckle filled the darkness. "With you, I'll never forget entering."

She laughed, but inside she was pretty damn pleased with herself. "So do it. Sleep."

"One more?"

"Are you kidding? I'm not even finished getting the shivers from the last one."

"Kiss, Jade." He demonstrated, so gently it made her insides mush. "Kiss."

"Okay. But just one."

''Yeah,'' he whispered as he turned them both on their sides and took her face between his hands. ''Just one.''

''NO, NO, I LOVE IT.''

''You liar. Your nose is getting longer as we speak.''

''It's not my nose.''

Jade whacked him in the shoulder. ''Ha, ha. I look horrible. If I'd seen what I really looked like last night, I would have run out and bought a wig.''

Max shook his head as he sipped his coffee. ''What do I have to do to convince you I'm telling the truth?''

''Nothing. You can't. I know you're being nice.''

''I'm not like that.''

She sat down with her own cup. They were both dressed, and the hair discussion had dominated the morning. ''Yes you are. You're terribly sweet, and you'd hurt yourself before you'd tell me the awful truth.''

''Boy, do you not know me.''

She reached over and took his hand in hers. ''That's where you're wrong, mister.''

His gaze moved to their hands. ''About last night. I never should have—''

''Forget it, Max. I'm a full-grown woman.''

''You can say that again.'' His grin lit his whole face, even his eyes. ''But I feel like I took advantage of you.''

She stopped in the process of fixing her own coffee. ''Really? I started it.''

''So, you took advantage of me?''

Jade sat opposite him. ''I'd say we both took advantage of an opportunity. It's just two adults in a situation. Don't read more into it than it means.'' She kept her expression neutral, not at all willing to have him guess that she'd spent an hour this morning going over and over last night, wondering if she'd been a fool.

She didn't think so, but she'd also never been in a situation remotely like this. Regardless, at the end of her hour of doubt she'd decided that what they'd done last night was dangerous but wonderful. Sex, in all its glory, not to be overblown or underappreciated. She'd also given herself permission to remember the best parts whenever she chose.

''It wasn't meant as an insult,'' Max said. ''I like you a lot. You're pretty damned amazing.''

Jade snorted in a very un-ladylike manner. ''Ah, you're just impressed that I got us home in one piece.''

''That's part of it.'' He sipped his coffee, but the way he looked at her wasn't exactly making it easy for her to concentrate on breakfast.

''What's the other part?''

He smiled. ''You're here. That's astonishing.''

''I know. Most people who heard you snore would have been out of here at the first opportunity.''

''That's not what I meant, and you know it. Besides, I don't snore.''

''Ha.''

''Uh, Jade, sweetheart, you don't want to go there.''

She brought her hand up to her throat. ''I do not!''

He nodded.

''Liar.''

"You're right. I'm lying like the rogue I am. You don't snore. You sleep like a dream."

"That's better."

He started in on his scrambled eggs, but he didn't stop grinning.

She hid her own smile behind her coffee cup.

"Basically," he said, "I'm saying that you're a pretty good date."

"You call this a date?"

"Ah. No. I guess not. But maybe when this is all over..."

Jade studied him. God, he was certainly handsome and his body—well, it wouldn't do to think about that when she had something else to do. Or his highly educated hands, either. She shook her head. "We should focus, Max. What're we doing today?"

He looked a bit disappointed when he leaned back, wincing slightly at the pain in his side. "I figured we'd call Peter, see if he found anything. Call Herb for the same. Get Patti's phone number, and see if she can give us the password on those files. She'll remember me."

"No kidding."

He didn't look amused at her joke. "I meant, as a friend to Werner."

"And then?"

Max shrugged. "We'll see where it takes us. We've still got to find the Geotech Cayman account, and how—if—they're coercing Senator Parker."

"Thanks for the 'if.'"

"I'm sorry, Jade. But you've got to admit—"

"I don't have to admit anything, and I still plan to

prove you're wrong.'' She got up from the table, and her sharp movements conveyed her anger.

They got ready to go, packing the laptop and the floppy disks, and headed through the heavy snow to the distant phone booth.

After the ''this is Frank'' introduction with Peter, they stood in the cold waiting for him to call back, and Max grabbed the phone on the first ring.

''I didn't really get anything of use from Edith Edwards,'' Peter began.

Max sighed. ''I expected as much, but I figured it was worth a shot. Her grandson say anything about me being there?'

''Where? At the Edwards?''

''I guess not.''

''You dumb son-of-a-bitch.''

''Yeah, but I did get a floppy out of it.'' He gave her a lopsided smile. ''No password though.''

''Maybe Mrs. Edwards can help. She certainly has no doubt you didn't kill Werner.''

''That's good to hear. I doubt she can help, though. I'll need Werner's secretary for that.''

Peter hesitated. ''Have you watched the news?''

''No. We...'' Max glanced at Jade, looking quite fetching with her blond hair tucked up under her baseball cap. ''We were kind of busy.''

''Patti Gellar's dead. Fell down the stairs at home.''

Max briefly closed his eyes, his blood running cold. Another senseless death. ''Right. Damned convenient.''

''So far there's no evidence of foul play. The police are calling it an accident.''

"Damn. I'll call you later, Pete." Max hung up and turned to Jade's querying glance. "Patti's dead."

"What happened?"

"Fell down the stairs. I've got to call Herb." As he turned back to the phone, she stopped him with a hand on his arm.

"Didn't you mention her to Herb the last time you talked to him?"

"God, you're right." His jaw clenched. "He was supposed to send someone to watch out for her. Stupid bastard was too worried about his job."

"What if he's in on it? What if he's been bought off by Geotech?"

"No way." Max shook his head, but doubt grew in his face.

"How well do you know him?"

"I thought I knew him well enough." He exhaled slowly, blindly staring at the cars stopped at the intersection, ignoring the annoying beep of the phone in his hand. "That's really reaching. I mean, why him?"

"I don't know. I just figured I should bring it up."

He rubbed his eyes. "If I've learned nothing else, anything is possible. He could have tracked the calls."

"I'm thinking Geotech is systematically trying to dispose of anybody or anything that can harm them. And getting away with it."

Thoughtfully, Max replaced the receiver. "Maybe you're right. I don't know who to trust."

They headed back to the warmth of the car and sat. Max stared out the window at the falling snow, not even reaching for the key.

Jade looked at him. ''Now what?''

''I don't know.''

''So we'll figure it out ourselves. We're reasonably bright, and our motivation is right up there in the life-and-death category, so failure isn't an option.'' She folded her arms across her chest. ''Right?''

Slowly, a smile crept onto his lips. ''Kind of funny hearing this from you.''

''Hey, I'm just sayin'.''

He laughed, but then his smiled faded. ''Thing is, I'm not the computer maven you'd think. In fact, I'm really not good with them at all. I've been known to screw up Tetris.''

''I'm no Bill Gates either, but I do know something about how people pick passwords. Let's go find a coffee shop and take the laptop in and figure it out. People dumber than us do it all the time. Well, dumber than you, anyway.''

''Cute, Parker. Cute.'' He frowned. ''Too dangerous to go to a coffee shop, though.''

''Not with our new golden hair. Besides it's better than sitting here and freezing our butts off. We'll be careful.''

He started the car and she directed him. She'd seen the coffee shop the last time she'd been in town, and it looked a little dingy. Which was perfect. And now with their new hair, the danger seemed minimal.

Inside, they found a booth near the back, sat next to each other, and ordered coffee. She didn't look at the waitress even once, but the woman seemed highly unconcerned with who they were. The coffee came right away, and when Max handed her a packet of sweetener, his fingers lingered on hers. It wasn't a big deal, but it felt like one. She got all fluttery inside, and it made her more determined than ever to crack the password.

She thought about her time with Mike, the last big relationship she'd had. There had been zero flutters. Even though she'd liked him, it had been more of an intellectual exercise than anything else. This was different. And yeah, maybe it was because of all the stuff going on in their world, but maybe it was just because she really liked this guy.

She stole a glance his way only to find him blatantly staring at her. The look in his eyes increased the flutters tenfold, and it was all she could do not to giggle like a teenager.

But now wasn't the time to get all puppy-love goofy. Nothing could happen between them until they were safe again. Until Geotech was exposed, her father was cleared, and Max was off the hook. So, to work.

Jade put the laptop on the table where they could both look at it and inserted one of the floppy disks they'd brought from Werner's.

"Okay. Most people use simple things they'll remember for passwords. It's why they aren't as effective as they could be."

Max nodded. "I usually just use my name."

"Exactly. Now, while you were asleep, I looked through the computer, and I tried Werner's wife's name, his daughter's and his grandson's, but none of them worked. It could also be a birthday or something."

He told her the date and she typed it in. No luck.

She sighed, avoided looking at the waitress while she ordered pancakes and Max ordered bacon and eggs. Once they were alone again, she thought about the article she'd read about passwords. "Did Werner have any favorite books?"

"I have no idea."

"Let's try some other stuff, like hometown or close friends."

"Oh, man."

"Unless you have a better idea…?"

Max sighed, and once again gave her various names he associated with Werner. Nothing worked. The meal came, and Jade continued to type in words, his address, his dog's name in between bites. Finally, in frustration, Jade closed the laptop.

"Let's just talk about him for a few minutes."

"I'm game. What do you want to know?"

She took a bite of her pancake, then asked, "What did he like? What were his passions?"

"Family. Business. Books. Movies."

"Well, we tried books. What kind of movies did he like?"

Max shrugged. "Classics, mostly. Jeez, he had hundreds of black and white films on tape. I don't think he watched anything made after 1950."

"What were his favorites?"

"Strangers on a Train. The Man Who Knew Too Much. He was nuts about Citizen Kane."

Jade's eyes widened. "Citizen Kane, huh?"

Max's heart speeded a bit as she opened the laptop up, inserted the disk again, and, at the password query, typed in "Rosebud." The disk whirred, and moments later, a list of folders appeared onscreen. She grinned like a kid Christmas morning.

"Well, I'll be damned."

"Bless you, Orson Welles."

He scanned the list of files.

Jade highlighted row after row. "Looks like they're arranged by date."

Max scrunched in close to her, peering at the screen. "Open one."

Jade clicked on the E-mail folder, and a series of document titles appeared. She opened one at random. They read it, then opened another. "They're all to and from Geotech."

They read a few, then closed the folder. The waitress came by and refilled their coffees, but Max wasn't interested. There was too much to go through on the laptop, and his patience was nil.

Jade scrolled down to her birth date, the day her father had gone AWOL, opened the folder, then the first e-mail. "Subject in Kendall," it read. "What's Kendall?" she asked.

"A town about thirty miles south of Colonial Beach."

"What's there?"

"As far as I know, Port Kendall Marina is the biggest in town. Open some more."

There were several unrelated inter-office e-mails, then "Operation *Irish Mist* a success. Will call later. R."

"That *Irish Mist* thing again," Jade said.

"In Kendall? Makes sense. We figured it might be a boat."

"And the 'R?' Could that be Retik?"

Max leaned back, a deep frown creasing his forehead. "Maybe. I don't know. But we could go up there and try to find it."

"It beats sitting here."

Max smiled at her. "Oh, I don't know." He put his hand on her thigh, liking that she didn't jump. That she smiled back.

Jade relished his touch, the closeness. But she punched his shoulder, dropped her grin. "Let's go, Lothario."

He didn't move immediately. Not even his hand. He looked as if he was going to say something, but then he didn't. He just nodded. Got his wallet out and paid the bill, leaving a nice tip for the waitress.

He drove. As they headed toward the coast, neither of them spoke. Jade was still wrapped in thoughts about her birthday and her father's absence. About what they would find once they got to their destination. She didn't like the worry in her gut, the fear that Max would find out something bad about her father. Not that she didn't believe in him, but no one was perfect, not even Senator Parker.

Finally, they turned off at the Kendall exit and headed toward the marina. "Whoa. This has sure grown since I was here last." Max looked around at the apartments and housing that had sprung up around Kendall.

"When was that?"

"Must be a good fifteen to twenty years. It was a

really rural little town then. Look at it. Hotels, apartments. All the new housing.''

''How far is the marina?

''Ten minutes, we'll be there,'' he said. ''Although what we'll find...''

He was thinking about evidence, of course. About finding something that would incriminate her father.

At the thought, her stomach tightened. As always, thoughts of her father made her crazy to let him know she was all right. There had to be a way of letting him know without tipping their hands. If they could figure out Rosebud, they could do anything, right?

The weather became increasingly dismal as they reached the road running along the water and followed it south. Three minutes later, they found themselves at the Port Kendall Marina, welcomed by a barely visible sign to the east and a stretch of shops to the west.

They eased the Taurus into a parking slot, by a Dumpster, so the car wouldn't be visible from most of the lot yet was still close to the dock. There was only one other car in the vicinity, which wasn't surprising given the eerie mix of fog and snow that engulfed the marina. ''Where do we start?'' Jade asked.

''We can't go through the harbormaster.''

''So, we wander around and act like tourists?''

''I'm thinking, yeah, although I'm not too worried about looking suspicious. Anyone'd be crazy to come out on a day like this.''

She got out of the car and shivered in the cold. Past the parking lot, the masts of the boats poked out of the fog that hugged the coastline.

It was going to be her second crack at breaking and entering, and it was scarier this time than the last. In the mist, the echoes of their footsteps sounded distant, like they were being followed. For all she knew, they were.

They could disappear into the icy Atlantic, and no one would ever know.

Chapter Eleven

She wasn't the largest yacht in the marina, but the *Irish Mist* was far from the smallest. From where they stood, looking up at the gunwales, they saw a forest of teak and mahogany, with brass fittings, disappearing into the fog. The name was in gold paint with black edging, all in Old English letters, across the stern.

They looked at the ladder, then at each other.

"Well…" Max said.

"Looks deserted."

"Yeah." He looked up and down the dock, then at Jade. "We won't get a better shot at this. Let's do it."

He climbed the ladder first, then looked down from some eight feet up and waved to Jade. She climbed, gripping the side rails with all her strength, not daring to look down, and feeling for all the world like she had a target painted on her back.

The fantail was shrouded not only in fog, but with a large white canvas cover, not unlike a sunshade over a large picnic table. Jade's gaze went right to a pair of double doors inset with stained glass, so beautifully etched they looked like something from a museum.

"Not your average weekend cruiser," Max said.

"Why are you whispering?" she asked, keeping her voice as low as his.

"'Cause I'm scared." He took her hand. "Come on, Hutch, let's get on with it."

Their footsteps echoed on the dark teak deck, then died in the fog as they walked to the doors. Max's glance met Jade's, and he reached for the brass handle, molded in the shape of a leaping dolphin.

"Should we worry about fingerprints?" she asked.

"The least of our worries." He pushed the handle down but it was locked.

"Damn."

Max held up one finger, then reached into his jeans pocket with the other. He pulled out a black leather case that looked to Jade like a manicure kit. He unzipped the thing and pulled out a tool Jade had only seen on television.

"I thought those were illegal."

"They are," Max said, as he bent on one knee in front of the lock.

"So how come you have one? And know how to use it?"

"Echoes of my sordid past. I'll tell you all about it once I get this door opened." He worked on it for several minutes, while Jade divided her attention between the Atlantic seaboard and Starsky.

When the latch finally clicked open, Max grinned, and she just shivered. "I'm not cut out for this, Max. I feel like I did when you were stalking me. You know, like there's someone out there, watching."

"They'd have to be able to see through all this fog," he said, "but let's get inside anyway." He pushed the heavy mahogany and glass doors open.

Except for the low ceiling, the room could have been mistaken for an upscale bar. A pair of long solid mahogany counters bracketed the sides of the room, backed by brass portholes which, on a sunny day, would probably lend a warm light to the entire space. There were a number of well-polished tables about the room, several with inlaid chessboards.

The teak flooring continued inside from the fantail, and the room was designed to work with the after deck as a sweeping dance floor when the doors were opened wide. A rosewood and mahogany bandstand had been built into the port side near the rear doors. Max pulled the doors closed behind them, the muted colors splashing eerily across the room.

Holding hands, they moved deeper into the room. "Wish I'd brought a flashlight," Max whispered.

Jade cleared her throat. "Look, Max. This is spooky enough without you whispering, okay? If anybody's onboard, they're going to hear us walking around anyway. If we're already screwed, I'd rather not have to strain to hear you."

"Sorry," Max whispered, then cleared his throat and, in a normal voice repeated, "Sorry. You're right. It's just..."

"Let's check out those doors." Jade pointed to the front of the room, opposite them.

They picked their way through the tables and stood in front of the rear bar, looking to the doors on either side.

"Should we split up?" Jade asked. She did not, however, let go of Max's hand.

At that moment, a particularly brutal wave pushed the boat against the bumpers hanging off the dock, and a loud, hollow bang rang through the empty interior, startling them both.

"If we're going to hang, let's hang together." Max pulled her toward the portside door. Pushing down on the brass dolphin handle, he opened the door and they entered a short passageway that led to a roomy, well-equipped galley.

"I've seen smaller kitchens in hotels," Jade said.

"They're obviously set up for partying." Max pulled her forward, and they moved through the gleaming stainless steel and aluminum fittings, past two six-burner stoves to the front of the room. Here their footsteps echoed harshly, as the deck was covered with metal plates instead of the wood behind them, and there were no portholes. Again, there were two doors out of the front of the galley, one leading straight ahead, and the other to starboard. Jade opened the door and peeked out. "Passageway," she said.

Max nodded and opened the other. "Same. Probably meet at the corner." He stepped through and she followed, and they went to the right and looked down the side passageway. Sure enough, there was the other door from the galley.

"It's starting to look like this deck is dedicated to partying," Max said.

"So where would people sleep?"

"They've probably got staterooms in the lower decks. The wheelhouse is another deck up. Big damned boat."

"That's for sure. But we still haven't seen anything suspicious. Unless you feel a luxurious yacht where a hundred people could party is a sign of too much money."

Max shrugged. "People who've earned their money should spend it as they please. I just wonder how Geotech earned theirs."

"Let's look down here." Jade pointed to the passageway running lengthwise next to the galley.

"Ballroom," Max said as he followed her to the next doorway.

As the passageway returned to the dark wood colors which were the predominant theme to date, the gloom seemed thicker. There were fancy brass lights mounted on the bulkheads, but since they were unlit, Jade had to feel her way along.

Max's fingers brushed across a switch and he flicked it, and suddenly the dim passageway burst into warm light, and they could see the door a few feet away. They reached it and went through.

The cold winter light filtering in from the portholes on the outside bulkhead stood in stark contrast to the lighted hallway, but now that Max knew the lights would work, he looked for a switch.

"I'm guessing this is the traditional smoke-filled room," Max said.

"My dad's library isn't this nice." Jade looked around, wide-eyed. Everything was done in dark-stained mahogany and rosewood. At the back wall, next to the door leading out to the ballroom, were bookshelves with glass doors that pulled out and down to protect hundreds of leather-bound volumes, and a large Persian rug lay on the floor with several leather chairs placed on it.

On the starboard side, beneath the brass portholes, were more bookshelves, while the front of the room had a wet bar. To either side and in front of the bar were small Persian rugs with leather overstuffed chairs on them, and more bookcases. The lighting was warm and indirect, except for above the single largest feature in the room—a massive octagonal card table, its top a small sea of green felt and the edges made of a dark-stained oak. There were comfortable-looking chairs at each position. A series of small spotlights shone on the table, with another shining directly down on the center.

"Nice place for a friendly card game," Jade said.

"Or a not-so-friendly card game."

She thought about her father as they headed for the doors behind the bar.

Inside, the room was empty. Just narrow paneled walls. No Persian carpets, no comfy wing chairs. Nothing.

"A passageway?" Jade asked.

"Maybe. We need a light."

She looked to her left while Max checked out the right. He found the inlaid switch. Once they could see clearly, he walked slowly down the wide corridor, examining the walls as he went. Jade wasn't sure what he was looking for, but couldn't help but notice him pressing the walls as he went. He paused halfway through, turning toward a particular section.

"I think I've found something."

She joined him just as the wall panel in front of him slid silently open, revealing a small surveillance room. It looked like something she'd see in Las Vegas, with a ton of monitors, each showing a different view of the boat, earphones on the stainless steel desks, two high-tech chairs, microphones on stands, the whole nine yards.

"Bingo," Max said.

"Good God, there are cameras in the bedrooms."

Max nodded as he walked in. "Audio, video. This stuff is state of the art, and it looks to me like there's not an inch of this place that's not being covered."

Jade's gaze went to the monitors on the left. "Max."

"Yeah?" he said, sounding distracted.

"Look at this."

She didn't turn, but she felt him next to her. His low whistle told her he'd seen what she was looking at. Crystal-clear views, on four cameras, of every position at the big poker table in the main salon.

"So this is how they got him."

Jade wrapped her arms around her waist. "Those bastards."

"Yeah," Max said. "Bastards. Let's see what kind of tape storage they have, shall we?"

"Oh, man, if we can get them cheating on tape, it'll…"

He squeezed her arm, gave her an encouraging smile. "Yeah, it will. But don't get your hopes up. It's doubtful they'd leave incriminating evidence."

Jade nodded and started opening cabinet doors while Max continued to figure out the controls. One cabinet contained another TV monitor and a control board, but on the next, she hit pay dirt. "I've got tapes. Lots and lots of tapes."

He moved next to her and whistled softly. Where everything else on the ship had been spotless and tidy, the tape cabinet was jumbled with haphazard VHS cases. As if they'd been tossed in hastily with no thought or plan, other than to stow them quickly. ''We'd better hurry,'' Max said.

The tone of his voice matched the nervous tension in her stomach. Geotech wasn't messy. They wouldn't just leave these here, even if they didn't hold anything more than proof that they taped the poker games. Something was fishy about this. It occurred to her, as they began searching through the piles of tapes, that if it was the perfect time for them to break and enter, given the weather and the lack of witnesses on the dock, it would be a perfect opportunity for Geotech to pay a visit. She kept tossing tapes, each of them labeled with a single date.

''See if you can find one with your birthday.''

Jade nodded, tight-lipped. Max was the one who found it. ''Let's pop this into a player.''

''Max, we have to get out of here.''

''We don't have a VCR at the cabin. It'll just take a second.''

He found the video player and inserted the tape, pressed play, then pushed buttons on the control panel until one of the monitors sprang to life with a panoramic shot of five men around the card table.

Senator Parker was in the center of the shot, and one of the other men was speaking to him. ''Senator. We're all honorable men. Of course we'll take your I.O.U.''

''I shouldn't do this,'' he said. And then he smiled. ''But what the hell, eh? I'm in.''

''That's the spirit, Senator.'' The figure turned toward the camera and beckoned to someone off screen.

''That's Retik,'' Jade said, although she couldn't take her eyes off her father.

''Sure is.''

They watched as a scantily clad young woman set a drink down next to the older man, who put his arm behind her back. The waitress jumped while the men at the table, including Senator Parker, grinned.

''Turn it off.''

''Jade...''

''I can't watch this. Turn it off and let's get the hell out of here.''

Max reached for the switch, then popped the tape out of the player. ''Okay, but we're taking this with us.''

She looked at him with tear-filled eyes. ''Oh, God.''

He folded his arms around her. ''I'm sorry, Jade.''

''I can't stand to see him like that.''

''We'll sort it out later. I promise.''

''Sort out what?'' She raised her face, tears streaming down her cheeks.

Max bent and kissed the tears away. ''It might not be what it seems.''

The boat rolled sideways heavily, and they almost lost their balance. Jade braced herself on the cabinet door.

''What the hell was that?''

''I don't know,'' Jade said as she pushed the eject button on the tape deck. ''But let's go.'' She put the cassette inside her jacket and zipped it up.

"Oh, damn," Max said, his voice back to a whisper.

She looked up, then followed his gaze to one of the top monitors on the other side of the room. A man stood to the left of the screen, on the dock, wearing a thick wool coat. He carried a valise in one hand, and something small in his other. Something smoking.

"Is that..."

Max nodded. "Retik."

"How did he find us?"

"I don't think he knows we're here."

As they watched, the man outside hoisted the smoking object high and to his right. The camera didn't follow the trajectory, but it was clear as hell where he'd hurled it.

The boat shook again, harder.

"Come on." Max grabbed her hand and yanked her out of the secret room, into the narrow passage. They ran into the main salon and were hit with thick, black smoke coming from the aft doors.

Max didn't hesitate. With her hand still firmly in his, he led her to the fore doors at a full run. They were outside in an instant, and then Jade was at the gunwales, gasping for air in the cold fog. She looked down at where the dock ramp was supposed to be. Only it was gone. "Uh, Max?"

He rushed over next to her and looked out at where the dock had been. They were floating away.

"Okay, then," he said. "Plan B."

Jade looked at him hopefully. "What is Plan B?"

"I have no idea."

Chapter Twelve

"Great. Now what do we do?"

Max looked at the dock, then at the fire blazing at the back of the ship. "Good question. We could either go up to the wheelhouse and radio for help, or try to get off."

"If we use the radio, this won't be very secret, will it?"

"No. It's probably not going to be a secret for very long anyway. Not with the fire. But at least we have the fog to hide us. You know the Coast Guard is going to come looking." Max bit his lip as he watched the tongues of flame licking up behind the wheelhouse. "And the way that fire's spreading, we might be in the water before they get here."

She looked down at the roiling sea. "I don't want to go in that water, Max."

"Relax, baby. It won't get to that."

She looked at him funny. Probably scared to death.

He turned around, checking out where they could still get to. "A boat this size has got to have a dinghy or lifeboats. With any luck, several. We have to split up." Although he didn't want to leave her. He pointed to the port side, where it was clearer. "You go down there. You're going to have to yell your head off if you find something. I'll go the other way."

She nodded. Turned, stopped. Then turned again, grabbed him by the shoulders and kissed him.

He wanted to kiss her back, but she was gone too quickly.

He watched her for a moment as she headed off, keeping her head down as she used the side gunwale to steady herself in the wildly unstable boat.

Damn, he needed to find a way off this boat. Max headed aft on the starboard side. When he looked back, he couldn't see Jade at all. Although on a clear day the smoke might have limited his vision, the fog itself was so thick he couldn't see more than a few feet anyway. He kept moving, and just when he figured he was going to get real wet, he stumbled across a davit with a wooden dinghy dangling from it. The fire was getting way out of hand, and he had to work fast. But first, he needed to get Jade.

He tore the canvas from the dinghy, saw that it did, indeed, have a large inboard motor, and he raced fore.

She wasn't far. In fact, she was almost exactly where they'd parted. "The fire," she said, having to almost yell over the noise of the flames. "I couldn't get anywhere."

"It's okay. I've found it. Come on." He pulled her so hard she slipped, and he caught her midfall, then helped her along until they reached the davit. The flames were nearly opposite them on the narrow gangway, and Max felt the heat on the back of his ungloved hands and his neck. "Climb in," he yelled. He held his hand out to help.

''What about you?''

''Got to lower the davit from here. Hurry.'' The rocking of the boat had increased to the point where, every few seconds, the dinghy was actually above the side of the boat instead of over the water. ''I think the boat's taking on water.''

''Fabulous. We're burning and sinking, is that it?''

''Just climb.''

She clambered into the rocking dinghy. ''Should I start the motor?''

He shook his head as he desperately searched first forward, then aft into the flames, for the ratchet mechanism that would lower the dinghy into the water. He found it, and jerked off the canvas cover, exposing the ratchet and crank.

''I'll lower the dinghy, then climb down,'' he yelled.

Jade nodded, clutching the side of the smaller boat.

Max cranked the dinghy down, timing it so he was lowering while the *Irish Mist* rolled to starboard, then winced when the dinghy slammed heavily into the side. Now he could feel the fire through his heavy coat, and the small hairs on the back of his hands curled from the heat. Still, he timed his cranking carefully. If he lowered the dinghy into the side of the *Irish Mist* he could lose both the dinghy and Jade.

After what seemed an eternity, the cables went slack. He looked over the gunwales to see the dinghy bobbing crazily on the water, Jade cupped her mouth. ''Should I release the cable?'' she called.

Max shook his head. He climbed on the gunwales and wrapped the hem of his coat around the cold and greasy cable, then grasped it and waited for the yacht to roll again.

When it once again rolled heavily to starboard, he took a deep breath and jumped from the gunwales, swung wildly into space for a few seconds, then slid as rapidly as he dared down the cable. Halfway down, the larger boat rolled the other way, and Max slammed into its side as the dinghy was pulled out of the water by the suddenly taut cable.

He grunted heavily as his wounded side came in contact with the hard wood of the yacht, nearly losing his grip, yet he was more afraid of the dinghy being damaged, and slid a bit more, trying to enter their only escape before the larger boat rolled again.

As his feet hit the bottom of the dinghy, the yacht rolled again, dropping the life boat into the water hard, and he nearly lost his footing as it rocked and splashed. He groped desperately for the hook, trying to release the cable before their only route to freedom was pounded against the bigger boat again.

With cold, bleeding fingers, he fumbled with the metal pin that held the cable securely to the hook. He pulled it loose seconds before the ocean sent a wave that would have crippled them.

Max turned his attention to the engine controls. The dinghy was large and had an inboard motor. He read the labels on the various switches and buttons, then flipped a switch and pushed a button.

The motor ground heavily, caught once, then died.

Max looked for the choke lever, found and pulled it, then pressed the button again.

This time the motor caught, coughed, caught again, then started with a powerful growl. Keeping a careful eye on the *Irish Mist*, he coaxed the engine with added gas and diminished choke until it was running smoothly. He engaged the screw and pulled away from the yacht, then steered against the current before he turned his attention to Jade. ''Are you okay?''

She was bent over the side of the boat and waved a hand back at him. ''I'm barfing, and if you offer to hold my hair, I'll kick you where it hurts.''

''Okay then.'' Keeping one eye on Jade, he steered the boat upstream, trying to head near shore at the same time. He looked back to see the stern of the burning yacht disappear into the fog like a dying ghost ship.

The dinghy bounced across the waves and Max tried going faster, then slower, in an effort to minimize the disturbance, but to no avail. When he slowed, the boat rocked more, so he settled into simply plowing ahead as rapidly as possible.

Jade pushed herself away from the side and struggled to join Max at the wheel. ''How're we doing?''

Max looked at her pallid face. ''Well, we're escaping. How are you?''

''I'm—''

But her words were lost in a roar of fire as the *Irish Mist* exploded. The blast tore through the weather, lighting the sky and the sea in red flames and debris.

''Hold on!'' Max screamed. ''Grab the side.''

Jade took hold of the boat, and so did Max, as they were hit broadside with a wave. The dinghy rose forever, tipping so far he was sure they were toast. All the while he was pelted with the debris, some of it still burning. At the last possible second, the wave passed them by, and the small boat dipped in the opposite direction.

Another wave hit, but it was smaller, and Max no longer believed they would drown. He wouldn't say the same for burning to death, however, as a big piece of flaming detritus missed his leg by a scant few inches.

He pulled his jacket sleeve over his hand and grabbed the wood, tossing it over the side.

Jade cried out, but when he looked up, she was all right, just scared to death. He didn't blame her.

The waves got less fierce, but it was no picnic on the water. His stomach roiled along with the sea as he tried to steer once more.

It took him way too long to get them to the dock. He was damn lucky he found it at all. The snow had thickened and visibility was near zero. No one had to come out to check the explosion yet, but Max knew it was likely a matter of minutes. Retik was nowhere in sight.

Max was just grateful they were alive and in one piece, although climbing up the dock was tricky given that his legs had turned to jelly.

Jade had gone ahead of him. She stood, arms wrapped around her waist, her eyes wide with fear. She looked like a ghost, and he felt like crap for dragging her into this nightmare. Only one thing to do.

"Well, that was fun," Max said, keeping his voice as light and casual as he could, as he led her toward the car. "What do you want to do now?"

She stopped stock still. Blinked at him, twice. "Are you crazy?"

"Definitely."

“We were nearly…” She looked down at her clothes, her jacket torn and burnt, her jeans no better, and both of them soaked. “It was…” Her gaze met his again. “It blew up.”

He smiled and pulled her into his arms. “Then what do you say we go home. Take a shower. Have some coffee.”

She nodded. Then stopped. Pulled back. “How's your side?”

“I'm okay.”

“Like hell. You're just in shock. Give you ten minutes in the car and you're going to fold like a cheap paper bag.”

Max held back his grin. This was better. Much better. “You're probably right. Think you can find your way back to the cabin?”

“Damn straight,” she said. “And let's hurry. Maybe Retik likes to stick around to admire his work.”

“Ah, good point.”

She pulled him closer as they made their way down the docks to the car, watching out for Retik, dodging behind the Dumpster as the first police car came screaming into the parking lot.

Jade just wanted to get home. To make sure Max wasn't going to die on her. Because she honestly couldn't take that. Not now. Not knowing…

She thought about the cold. About getting the keys from Max. About making sure he was buckled up and that the heater was turned on full-blast. She waited until the police had gone down to the docks to check the burning boat, then drove away as quickly as the bad road conditions allowed.

It took forever, what with the snowfall and the ice on the roads. Thankfully, the heater worked great, and Max fell asleep quickly. She, on the other hand, continued to shake, and not from the cold.

Retik had almost killed them. Again. And this time, he'd gotten just as close. A few minutes later…

She gripped the wheel tighter, focused everything she had on the road. Something had to give, and unfortunately, that something looked to be her father. How had he gotten on that boat? He'd led a whole secret life away from her. In order to fund gambling, he'd have to have gotten a new bank account, one she didn't know about.

But she had an idea where she'd find it. Her father had a private computer in his home office, one only he used. He didn't think she knew the password, but she did, although she'd never used it. If he'd kept any records, they would be there.

What was even more important was that he also kept something of a journal on that machine. Nothing regular, nothing that would even be considered a journal by most people. Notes, dates, thoughts. It was his garbage bowl, as he liked to call it, where he tried to empty his brain when it got too full.

Maybe, if she read that, she could understand.

It just made her so damn sad. If only people understood the good he did. But they wouldn't care. A person like her father wasn't allowed to make mistakes.

She continued to think and cry and shiver as she drove more and more slowly and the snow continued to build. By the time she pulled the Taurus into the garage, a full-scale snowstorm was raging, and Jade coaxed Max inside while she closed the garage.

He went directly to the heater, then to the coffee pot, not even stopping to take off his wet coat. When he measured the coffee, his hands shook.

She got her coat off, pronto, putting the hated video tape on the small table.

As fresh tears welled, she blinked them back, refusing to drown now that she was so far from the ocean. ''Mmm,'' she said, determined to be cheerful, to not let him see how finding that tape had shattered her world. It wasn't his fault. He had his own life to save. ''Good idea, coffee. But get the hell in the bathroom and get out of those wet clothes. I have to check your bandages.''

He shook his head. ''You first.''

''Tell you what.'' She walked over to him, tossed her cap on the chair, shook out her damp hair. Then she pulled his coat off him, making him switch the coffee scoop from hand to hand. The second he finished and pushed the button, she turned him around.

''What are you doing?'' he asked, although surely even he could figure it out after she undid his top button. ''I told you to shower first.''

She shook her head. ''Better idea.''

He fully understood when she pulled him toward the bathroom. ''Ah, two birds?''

She grinned. ''One stone.''

''I like the way you think.''

''It's purely medicinal,'' she said, as she closed the bathroom door behind them. ''You need to get out of those wet clothes.''

Max wasn't about to argue. He was tired, sore, way

the hell out of his league, and Jade was the best thing that had happened to him in a long, long time. Lousy timing in general. Extraordinary timing at the moment.

She seemed intent on divesting him of his wet clothes. Every time he tried to return the favor, she batted his hand away.

"What happened to the whole two birds thing?"

She smiled, her teeth still chattering. "You go in first and get the temperature right."

He nodded, but while she worked on unzipping his jeans, he watched her more carefully. While he loved the idea of sharing a shower with her, he wasn't convinced that her motive was purely lascivious. In fact, her movements were jerky, uncoordinated, and it wasn't cold enough in the bathroom for her to be shaking so violently.

She hadn't reacted this way the last time they'd almost been killed. Maybe this was a delayed response, post-traumatic shock.

Then he remembered the tape. Hell. Her whole world had collapsed on that boat. The man she'd idolized had gone up in flames before her eyes. There was no doubt anymore that Parker was involved with the Geotech scam, and he wasn't going to get out of it with a slap on the wrist. How involved was still to be determined, but the tapes along with his voting record didn't look good.

Werner had been right. And Jade had been dead wrong. It had to be killing her.

She tugged his pants halfway down his legs, and he grabbed her shoulders. "Jade."

Shaking him off, she bent down again to finish the

job, and he decided to let her. He wanted to calm her, and his chance would come once they were both in the shower. In fact, he helped, stepping out of his jeans and shorts, and kicking them to the side.

She stared at him, wide-eyed, strangely beautiful with her blond hair wild, her lips almost as pale as her cheeks.

He did just as she'd asked, got into the shower and got the water to the perfect temperature. When he peeked behind the shower curtain, she was mostly undressed already, with just her bra and panties still on. He watched her struggle with the bra, almost bursting into tears as the clasp remained stubborn. Finally, it was off, and then her panties joined his clothes.

Max opened the curtain for her and she climbed in.

He put her under the lion's share of the spray, wanting to warm her. She hugged herself, hunched forward, looking up at him like a wounded kitten, and his heart just goddamn broke.

"Come here," he whispered, folding her in his arms.

She pressed against him, and he could feel the tremors wrack her body. He wanted to say something, make it all better, but what the hell could he say? Her father was guilty. He'd betrayed his office. Effectively, his career was over. The hell of it was, he believed Jade when she said he was basically a good man. But even good men can do stupid things.

Jade kissed his shoulder, then the side of his chest. She broke free of his grasp, wanting instead to hold him steady, to keep him still, but he wasn't going to let her.

"It's okay, baby," he said, bringing her in close once more. "I know, I know."

She struggled, fought with him to let her go, but he held tight, talking to her gently, as he would a wild creature, letting her know she had someone to lean against, someone who would catch her when she fell.

And finally, she did fall. Hard.

It was as if all the bones in her body gave up at the same time, and the only reason she didn't crumple to the bottom of the tub was his hold on her. The shaking changed. It wasn't the tremors of shock, but a great release, an outpouring of sadness that went all the way to her soul.

She spoke, but the words were unintelligible, her mouth against his chest. But he knew what she meant.

"It's okay, baby. Let it out. I won't lie to you. It's going to change. But that doesn't mean you can't still love him. That he doesn't love you."

She just cried harder, still against his chest, her tears mingling with the warm water from the shower.

"You've been magnificent, you know that?" he said. "Brave and smart and just incredible. And damn it, I'm sorry it couldn't be better for your dad, but the truth was going to come out somehow."

She pushed away from him. Looked right at him. Her wet hair dripped, her eyes were red-rimmed and swollen. "My father is the best man I've ever known," she said, her voice gruff and thick. "He never would condone killing anyone. He wouldn't do that. He wouldn't do any of it."

Max didn't know what to say. She wanted to believe so badly. "We'll figure it out, Jade. We will."

"Damn right, we will," she said. "I will. I know

him. I know he had to have been coerced. There's no way he could have done this in his right mind.''

''Okay. Okay. We'll keep digging. I promise. But right now, we have to get you warm. Get you into bed.''

She put her hand up to her mouth, looked at his sopping bandage. ''Oh, God. I didn't even—''

''It's okay. I'm not bleeding. Sore, but not bloody. Let's just wash, okay? I've never washed blond hair before.''

Her gaze softened. She took a deep breath, then reached for the soap. ''Here.''

He took the soap from her hand, and after a brief kiss, he worked up a lather between his hands. She turned around, and he started washing her, from the top of her smooth back to the dimple above her round buttocks. Her muscles relaxed before his eyes as he ministered to her, rubbing the lather into her warm skin.

She turned then, looked up into his eyes. Leaning forward, she took his lips in a kiss, and this one wasn't so gentle. He felt her hand move down his belly. ''I don't want to think anymore,'' she whispered.

Max groaned when he pulled back. When he gripped her arms so she couldn't move down to touch his hardening length. ''No,'' he whispered, and turned her back around.

She tried to turn back, struggled, but he kept her still. Then she looked back at him, her eyes pleading.

''Trust me,'' he said.

Even though the water was still running, it hit her just below her chin so he could watch the tear make its way down her cheek, where it melded with another drop.

"Trust me," he said again.

She nodded once, faced front, her shoulders sagging.

He got the shampoo and poured some in his palm. After rubbing his hands together, he went to work lathering her hair, the blond still slightly disorienting. When the shampoo made everything slippery, he massaged her head, concentrating on her temples, moving gently, easily, relaxing one of the most sensitive areas on the body.

When she moaned, he knew he was doing it right. That he'd taken her from that wicked edge of desperation. But there was still a long way to go. She was wound as tight as a box spring. Guilt welled in his gut, but he ignored it, concentrating completely on Jade. She was the important one.

He continued to rub, using the pads of his fingers, until her head bobbed, until she had to put her hand on the shower stall to keep herself upright. Only then did he pick up the soap again, and wash her as if she were a child.

She allowed him to guide her, turning when he said, letting the water rinse her clean from head to toe. Then he had her stand still, water pouring on the back of her head, her eyes closed, while he used the soap on himself, washing in record time. He rinsed, then turned off the flow. Instead of making her step out into the cooler bathroom, he pulled two towels, the new ones she'd bought, from the rack. The first, he wrapped around his waist, wincing as it made contact with his bandaged side. The second, he used first to dry her hair, then turning it around on her body, making sure every part of her was dry.

He couldn't help his reactions to her naked flesh, to her incredible beauty, but he kept on task, ignoring the pull to touch her more intimately. He continued to nurse her as she'd done for him. To care for her as if her wound was visible.

Max stepped out of the shower. "Wait here."

He got her robe from the back of the bathroom door, and slipped it on her shoulders. She put it on the rest of the way.

He put his own robe on, but when she tried to leave, he stopped her. "Sit," he said, nodding at the commode.

She obeyed, as listless as the damp towel. He got the hair blower she'd picked up at the store and her hairbrush. Careful not to hurt her, he brushed and dried her hair. It was a slow process, which was good, calming. Her eyes closed almost immediately, and she rocked, arms crossed over her chest, as the sound of the dryer filled the room.

When he turned off the dryer, she opened her eyes. Looked up at him. "Let's have some of that coffee," he said.

She nodded.

She led him into the main room, but he steered her toward the bed instead of the kitchenette.

"I can do it," she said.

"I know. But I want to. You just get into bed, okay?"

"What time is it?"

"Night," he said. He kissed her cheek before he went to get the mugs.

He heard the sheets rustle while he fixed her cup. After putting the cream back in the fridge, he brought both mugs to the bed.

She took hers, smiled. At least, tried to. But her sadness sat heavy, weighing her down.

He settled beside her, not getting under the covers. "You want to talk?"

She shook her head.

"You want to listen?"

Again, she shook her head. Her gaze moved to his side. "What I want to do is change your bandages."

"I'm fine."

She handed him back her cup, without a sip missing. "Shut up and take your robe off."

He didn't argue.

Jade gathered the supplies, and then went all business on him. Taking off the old bandage, checking out the wounds, putting on the new. She moved smoothly, no more trembling. Nothing but the competent woman he'd come to know. The frightened child hadn't disappeared, though. She was just hiding.

After she put the last piece of tape on his side, her hand stilled. "I keep thinking I'm going to wake up," she said, so softly he had to strain to hear. "I mean, who really gets kidnapped. By Santa Claus, for God's sake. And then the cabin, and Retik, and all the cloak-and-dagger stuff. It doesn't happen to real people."

Her gaze shifted from his side to his eyes. "You don't happen to me."

"Come on up here," he said, taking her hand and pulling her back on the bed. "It is surreal as hell. I can't believe it half the time."

"I'm through the damn looking glass," Jade said,

staring past his shoulder now. At nothing. "Following a white hare. And nearly getting my head chopped off for my trouble."

"I'm sorry, Jade."

She nodded. "I don't blame you. Your life is at stake. What they did to you is inexcusable."

"But?"

She bit her lower lip. "I don't know who I am anymore. Nothing's the same. It's like someone took an eraser to my life, got rid of everything I could count on, and started scribbling in horrible things. What the hell happened? I know my own father, I've lived with him since I was eight, worked with him for years." Her gaze rose, pleading. "He's a good man. He never takes the easy way out. He fights for what's right. I swear to God, he couldn't do these things."

Max didn't feel it was the time to remind her about the tape. She knew. Accepting it was going to take some time, however.

"I..."

"What?" he asked, touching her arm.

She looked down at the connection. "I want my old life back. I want all of this to be a nightmare, and dammit, I want to wake up."

Max felt slapped. She wanted it all gone? Him, them?

None of it was her fault. He'd abducted her, and she had every reason to hate him for it. He'd been the one to expose her to the truth of her father, so what did he expect? Gratitude?

And yet...

He coughed, pushed down the disappointment in

his chest. She was the one who'd been blindsided. She was the one who mattered. ''He's still your father. This doesn't erase any of the good things he's done. He still loves you. He just made some bad choices.''

''Bad choices?'' She pulled back, lifted the comforter above her waist. ''He gambled with those people. Drank with them. He lied to me.''

Max wasn't the least bit sure of what he was doing. He should have let it alone, not helped her get upset again. He'd pulled her into the morass, and everything that she was feeling was his fault. If he could take it back, he would. But it was too late. He'd hurt her. Almost gotten her killed. What he felt for her was his own damn problem.

''The thing is,'' Jade said, her voice a whole lot softer, ''I'm so, so sad. He must have hurt so much. And I was there. I was with him, and I never knew. Maybe I did, but I didn't want to admit it. I never asked him where he was on my birthday, even though I knew he lied to me. If I had, this whole thing—''

Max put his hand on the back of her neck and pulled her gently forward. ''Jade, look at me.''

She didn't.

''Jade.''

Her gaze met his.

''This is not your fault. You did nothing wrong. He's a grown man. He made choices. You aren't his keeper, you're his daughter.''

''But he loved my mother so much. She was his everything.''

''Loss happens. And then we have to move on. I'm

sorry your father did what he did, but you're not to blame.''

''I—''

He moved closer to her. Moved his hand down her back. ''He's going to need you more than ever. And it's going to be hard as hell. But you know what? You can do it. I know you can, because I've seen what you're capable of. You're the strongest woman I know. Hell, you're the strongest person I know. You've faced impossible things with so much courage....'' He couldn't talk for a minute. The words stuck in his throat.

She shook her head, and then she leaned forward, kissed him with such tenderness, he didn't know what the hell to do.

So he kissed her back.

Chapter Thirteen

Jade melted into his arms. She let it all go, everything, except for the feeling of hands on her back, the sweetness of his lips. Nothing existed outside this room, this bed. It was all she had to hang on to, and she blessed him a million times for the sanctuary.

He pulled her tighter. She parted her lips, waiting for him to come inside her. He obliged, teasing her with his wicked tongue. She had learned his taste, the way he liked to fill her, then retreat, only to fill her again. It wasn't the exploration of before, but a familiar dance.

While she sparred with him, moaned against him, she ran her hand down his chest, below his waist.

What waited for her there was a promise. He was hot, ready, and when she circled him with her palm, his sharp gasp tickled her lips.

He pulled back, not quite disturbing her hold, and slipped her robe off her shoulders. Then he kissed her neck, nipped the skin, making her gasp, but instantly, his tongue was there, soothing her. He moved down to the curve of her shoulder, nuzzling, while his hand cupped her breast, lifting the weight of it, then rubbing her sensitized nipple with the flat of his hand.

She wanted no light teasing tonight. Nothing tame. Taking his hand away, she took the tip of her own nipple between her finger and thumb, squeezing it just hard enough to make herself moan.

A quick study, Max eased her away and took over, and his touch was infinitely more thrilling, because she didn't know what he'd do. Not one to waste the moment, she went back to her previous exploration, loving the feel of the heat and hardness of his desire.

The robe puddled at her waist, and she wrangled her hands free so she could get to his whole body, to play and play as long as she wanted. To drown in the man.

He let go but only so he could pull her legs to the bottom of the bed, stretching her out, flinging the robe on the floor, along with his.

Naked, the chill air a sharp contrast from the heat of their bodies, his hands were everywhere, running down her tummy, pausing briefly at her belly button, only to move down while his tongue darted into the tiny indent.

It tickled, and she grabbed his hair with both of her hands, tugging him up.

He looked at her, wild-eyed, so different with the pale hair, the dark stubble that had just scratched her stomach.

"Do everything," she whispered, not wavering her gaze an inch.

He moaned, then pulled himself free, moving down her body as he spread her thighs with his hands. He didn't let her go there, either. He lifted her legs, bent her knees, so her feet were flat on the bed. Then, with a laugh that gave her head-to-toe gooseflesh, he bent his head.

She couldn't reach him so she grabbed the comforter tight in her fists. With her eyes closed tight, her whole concentration was focused on his every move. A gentle brush of fingers through her dark curls. A breath, slow and long. Hot and cool at the same time.

She arched, raising her chest, as she felt the intense magic of his tongue. God, the way he moved. Languid, easy, as if he owned her, and he did. She was his, every part of her, as he circled her sensitized bud.

He didn't vary the pressure, so she had to, using her hips, her muscles. He dipped, licked, circled, playing her like an instrument. And she couldn't stay quiet, not while he was making her insane.

''Please,'' she said, not even sure what she was begging for. But he knew. Because she felt a finger at her center, slipping inside her, easing apart her soft folds. He pushed, hard, once, then again, never stopping with his mouth, only now he'd captured her between his teeth, and he used furious suction to take her to the moon.

She pulled the comforter from the sides of the bed, one fold covering half her face, but she didn't care. She was screaming, flying with his tongue and his fingers, with all the electricity in the sky, all right there, in her center, in her whole body.

He gave her no time to come down. A heartbeat passed, then he was leaning over her, guiding himself into her. He paused. She learned to breathe again. And then he was in her, all the way in her, filling her completely, pulling out until she was almost empty, then in. Hard. Hard.

This time her release made the room spin, her body leave the bed, her cry become a scream. Still, he went on, with a ferocity that would have scared her if she'd had any awareness other than her own pleasure.

When he stopped, up to the hilt inside her, she opened her eyes to see his grimace, the intensity as fierce as a wild animal, only his eyes were open, too, staring into hers, burning into hers.

Time slipped. Stretched. Then, with a glorious tremor, she tumbled back down to earth, to his arms. He groaned from deep in his chest and when he collapsed, he was wet and heavy, and that was so very, very good.

It took a long time for her to calm down. A longer time to be able to move with any kind of grace. But when she could, she petted him, long strokes down his back, her hand rising and falling with his every breath.

"I'm sorry," he said. "I'm crushing you."

She held him down with her palm. "No. Don't move. Stay right there."

"How can you breathe?"

"I'm fine," she said. "That's a lie. I'm..."

"Yeah," he said, but the word was mostly air. "Only, it's cold in here, and I want you under the covers."

"I don't care."

"I do. You need to be warm."

She laughed, softly. "I think one of us is cold, and it isn't me."

"Okay, okay. Busted."

She kissed him before she let him move. He kissed her back the second he'd rearranged the covers. Pulling her close so they touched from shoulder to knee.

"That was amazing," he said.

"I'm thinking World Book of Records."

"Oh, yeah."

"And now, I think, sleep," she said.

"Again, I concur."

She giggled, kissed his nose. "You surprise me, Max Travis."

"Oh?" He managed to open one eye, raise one brow.

"I didn't know newsmen were such stud muffins."

"They aren't. Just me. And Ted Koppel, but that doesn't leave this room."

She laughed, marveling that he could do that to her. Make her fly, make her scream. Make her laugh. Especially after the day she'd had. But then, that was his gift. At least, his gift to her.

JADE WOKE EARLY. The sun was just coming up above the tree line, filling the room with timid shadows. She moved carefully, not wanting to disturb Max, but it was hard not to moan from the protestations of her muscles. Everything hurt, and she blamed that bastard Retik and Geotech. She blamed them for everything, and if it was the last thing she ever did, she'd make them pay.

But for now, she needed coffee. After a quick trip to the bathroom, where she tied her weird blond hair back in a ponytail and put on jeans and a thick sweater, she got just that. Surprisingly, the heady aroma of the coffee didn't wake Max, which was a good thing. He needed to rest. She needed to get the hell out of this cave.

She waited impatiently until she could steal a full mug from the pot, then drank it sitting at the table, staring at the video tape and the laptop. The thought of destroying them both crossed her mind, but fleetingly. It was too late for that. No matter what, unless she and Max were both murdered, the truth was going to come out.

Thinking about how closely they'd come to just that, she shivered, images of the exploding boat flashing in her mind's eye. God, they'd nearly…

She stood, got her coat, which thankfully was dry, gloves and her baseball cap, donning them all with rough jerks and quick zips. Then she went out the front door into the middle of winter.

The storm from yesterday had dropped several inches of snow, which would make driving hell, but looked incredible. A deep breath of icy air filled her lungs with strange fire, but it felt damn good.

She looked over at her tree. It would be work to get there today, but work was just what the doctor ordered. Her boots weren't designed for the job, but she didn't care if she got snow in her socks. She didn't care about much.

By the time she touched her gloved hand to the side of the freezing trunk, she was winded. And her mind was made up.

This was it. No more hiding. No more running. Today, she would go home. The truth wasn't going anywhere, and the longer she put it off, the more terrifying it would become.

She looked back at the cabin. It seemed so small

and innocent, as if some giant hand could shake it up like a snow globe. Inside was a man she'd come to care for. More than she'd even realized. Until this morning, when she knew she wouldn't see him again.

Blinking back tears that held as much anger as sadness, she folded her arms across her chest, shifted her position to be away from the biting breeze. It wasn't fair. None of it was. But so what?

Fair had disappeared when a scraggly Santa Claus brandishing a gun had come along. Fair had died with her mother. All that was left was what she had to do.

Take care of her father. Stand by his side when his ship exploded and sank, just like the *Irish Mist*.

They would lose it all, and for her dad, the worst of it was going to be the humiliation. God, he was so proud of the work he did, of the good things he championed. To have that stripped away would leave him so vulnerable she wondered if he'd survive it.

Well, he had to. Just like she had to go back home, convince him to tell the police, tell the Senate Oversight Committee, everything. His gambling, the account in the Cayman Islands, the bribe.

Just thinking about it made her sick to her stomach. Because she had to get her father to come forward before Max wrote his story. And Max had to write his story fast, because if he didn't, he'd be arrested for murder and kidnapping. Which wasn't going to happen.

It all had to come together like a category five hurricane. Her father's confession, the information that Peter had, and of course Max's story. Once it broke, all their lives would be catapulted into another dimension. One she could hardly bear to think about.

Especially the part where she couldn't see Max.

It wouldn't work. No matter how she tried to bend it or stretch it, them being together, seeing what their lives could be together, wasn't in the cards.

Max had to write his story. And his story would crush her father. Yeah, she loved Max, but she owed her Dad. Owed him everything. She wouldn't turn her back on him now. Or ever.

So this was it. The end of one chapter, the beginning of another. When all she wanted was a story with a happy ending.

The wind had picked up, and she was starting to get seriously chilled. It took her longer to get back, probably because she had no desire to face what had to be faced inside.

But she opened the door anyway, to find Max, in his bathrobe, looking sexy and disheveled at the table, drinking coffee.

"I'm really glad you came back," he said. "I was afraid I was going to have to find a St. Bernard. What, were you building a snowman?"

She smiled, missing him already. "Nope. Just making a plan."

His right brow lifted, and she wanted to kiss him. "Oh?"

She shed her heavy outer garments, and switched her boots for slippers. Then she joined him at the table. "We're going back."

"Back?"

She nodded. "Home. It's over Max. You have enough evidence now to clear yourself. To implicate Geotech. And my father."

"Whoa. What the hell happened out there?"

"Nothing. Except reality. It's time. Only, I have a favor to ask you."

He put his hand on hers. It was warm and kind, and she couldn't let it stop what she had to do. "I want to talk to my father first. Convince him to confess before your story hits the papers."

"Sure. Yeah, of course, but aren't we rushing things here? I mean, that one tape might not be the whole story. There are probably mitigating circumstances. And what about Herb? We don't know if he had anything to do with Patti's death—"

She slipped her hand from under his. Put her finger to his lips. "It's over. And we're going home. So I suggest we pack now. Who knows when the weather will turn too ugly to drive. I can't do this one more day."

He didn't say anything for a long time. Even when she got up and poured herself another cup of coffee, he just sat there, staring at her chair.

She wouldn't rush him, because she knew he had to process it all, just as she had. And that he'd come to the same conclusion. That their time together was at an end. Even though all she wanted was to spend time with him in the real world. Go to dinner. The movies. She wanted to see his horrible apartment, and find out everything about his job. She had a feeling she would have really liked his father.

But none of that mattered now. The course was set, and she'd better not put it off any longer.

She put her cup on the table, and went to the bathroom to gather her things. She had no luggage, so paper sacks would have to do. There were some under the sink. On her way there, Max stopped her with his hand on her arm.

"Wait."

"I can't. We can't."

"You have to."

She looked down at him, at his troubled gaze. "Okay," she said quietly. "Sure."

He watched her sit, then leaned forward. "What happened to you out there?"

"What did you think we were going to do? Wait until Retik finally got the job done? Right now, we're the only thing standing between him and the truth. If he kills us, Geotech carries on with their bribery and their murders. My father continues as the head of the Ways and Means committee. No one's the wiser."

"Yeah."

"You think I would let him do that? Live with that kind of guilt?"

"So you're saying the shame is easier?"

"No. But it's better."

Max nodded. "Now it's about his soul."

"Prosaic, but yes. It is. Like I've said, I know my father. And if he doesn't come clean about this, it'll kill him. I've already lost one parent too many, thank you."

"You think he'll agree? Just like that?"

She nodded. "It won't be that simple, but yeah. In the end, he will. Because he's not an evil man. Because he believes in the principles of this country. I'm sure he's sick about what he's done, and it's not helping that I disappeared. He needs me, and I'm going to be there for him."

"I can make it look better in the paper—"

She recoiled in her seat. "No. What, have I been talking in Greek here? The man who adopted me, gave me a life beyond my wildest dreams, is all about integrity. This…aberration…is all about pain and confusion, not changing the rules. You have to tell the truth, Max."

"We don't know the whole truth."

"So we'll find out. Together. And that's what you'll print."

He nodded. Looked at his hands. "And after?"

She'd dreaded this part. But it was only the first of many horrible things she'd have to face in the upcoming hours and days. "There won't be an after. Not for us."

He raised his head, his eyes filled with a pain that mirrored her own. "No."

She smiled sadly. "It can't be anything else. You know that as well as I do."

"Okay, so we can't see each other for awhile, but all this will die down. It'll be over, forgotten, yesterday's news."

"Not to my father, it won't."

He opened his mouth, then shut it again, pressing his lips tightly together.

"I don't like it either." She leaned forward, gathering his hands in hers. "I won't lie. I hate this. You've been…" She shook her head. "To say you've been a surprise would be an understatement. The last thing on earth I expected was to fall in love with the man who kidnapped me, but guess what?"

At her words, his face crumpled into a mask of hurt. "Oh, God."

"Yeah," she said. "I couldn't agree more. But, it's

our lousy luck, Mr. Travis, that you have to go on to win a Pulitzer, and I have to take care of my sick father. He is sick, you know."

"I do. I know that."

"So write that. Let people know what good he's done. Don't let them remember only this."

"I promise."

"You'd better."

He leaned forward and kissed her lips. "I love you," he whispered.

"I know," she said. Then she stood up, because she had to do something fast, before she fell apart. "Let's get going. There's a lot to pack, and it's almost ten."

Max went through the motions, taking only what was pertinent, leaving most of what he'd bought. He'd come back to the cabin and clean it out later. He made sure he had his computer, all the Geotech papers, and of course the tape.

Because he wasn't at all sure his introduction back into society wouldn't be a messy business, he put the gun in his jacket pocket.

He watched Jade as she cleaned, straightened, packed her things into paper bags. He hated the haunted look on her face, the dark circles under her eyes.

God, she was so beautiful. Yeah, he liked her other hair color better, but even as a blonde, she broke his heart.

He put his jacket behind the chair. Jade was folding the comforter. Her hands, lovely and slim, were competent and quick, each movement graceful. When she bent to get the pillow, his gaze swept the curve of her back, the length of her legs. He still wasn't convinced that it had to end between them. So all right, her father wasn't going to be his biggest fan, but dammit, Max hadn't made him do any of the things he'd done.

He was only the messenger. And everyone knows what happens to the messenger.

Max turned away, thoroughly disgusted with the whole situation. He'd taken Jade as a last ditch effort to save his life. Never in a million years would he have guessed that things would turn out this way. That he would care more about her than the truth.

Maybe…?

He sat down heavily, put his head in his hands. There was no way to hide this, bury it, turn the smoking gun into a rose petal. And it was clear Jade wasn't going to budge from the senator's side.

Which was honorable as hell, but he didn't particularly care about honor. Dammit, he loved her. He'd never loved anyone like this in his life, never dreamed it would happen to him. Not him. And it was all going to melt away a hell of a lot sooner than the snow outside.

"Is there anything else?"

He looked up. Jade had her coat over her arm. She wore clothes he'd bought her, before he'd even known that she was braver than the toughest marine. Her face was clean, no makeup, nothing fancy or artificial to get in the way of who she was. And he'd never seen anyone more beautiful. "No, I've got everything."

"I think you might want to just throw out that comforter," she said. "I doubt the blood will come out. And don't forget all that trash in the garage."

He nodded. "Later."

"Yeah."

"So what's the plan?"

"We go to my house. I'll call my dad, ask him to meet me there. After we've talked, I'll come get you. We'll call the police together."

"I don't think I can just sit in the car."

"I won't let you get caught. There's room for the car in the back." Her mouth quirked on one side. "Besides, no one will even recognize you, Blondie."

"Look who's talking."

Her hand went to her ponytail. "I'd always wondered what it would be like."

"And?"

She shook her head. "It's not for me."

"It doesn't matter what color your hair is," he said, standing. He walked over to her, took her hand in his. "You're the most—"

She turned, sharply. "Oh, God, you can't. Please don't say anything wonderful."

He had to laugh, although he felt more like crying. "Okay. Nothing wonderful."

She turned back with a smile and watery eyes. "Let's go."

He nodded. Picked up his case and his laptop. "I'll get the car started. Open the garage."

She picked up one of the paper bags. "We'll load everything in the trunk, then do a walk-through."

"Right."

Jade smiled at him. "You aren't moving."

He looked at her, as deeply as he could, trying like hell to memorize every inch of her face. The green of her eyes, the arch of her brows, the symmetry that made the whole package a work of art. "I hate this," he said. "I just found you."

She closed her eyes, then came up to him, real close. Reached up and kissed him softly. "I'll never forget you. Not ever."

"Jade—"

She stepped back. "You promised."

He gripped his bag tighter, because what he wanted to do was trash everything in sight. Except her. Her, he wanted to protect, to keep. Her, he wanted to love. "Yeah," he said. "I promised." Then he turned and headed for the car.

Behind him, he heard her whisper, "Merry Christmas, Max."

He'd forgotten. It was Christmas. He should be happy. Soon, he'd have his life back. His reputation. He could walk freely among men. And still, it was the lousiest Christmas in the history of the world.

Chapter Fourteen

Even the drive back felt different. She kept looking at the people in the cars, wondering about their lives, what brought them out on Christmas Day. Had they had a warm, cozy morning, filled with presents and cookies and ornaments? Or were they off to visit family, to gather together for a fine holiday feast? All of them had more to look forward to than she did.

She hummed ''Silent Night,'' but only the first bar. Then she turned to look at the blond man driving. Max. No one named Max should have blond hair. He was still handsome, though. Nothing he could do to disguise that. Handsome and sweet, and the way he made love to her was a gift she'd never expected. But it was all fading with every slow mile toward home. Toward her father's house. The house she had been so ready to leave.

That wouldn't be happening. Not for a long time. And she might as well forget about her thesis. Standing by her father would be a full-time job. There would be hearings, attorneys, court appearances, the media. Nightmare, nightmare, nightmare, and she would have to smile, be strong, not let the cracks show.

It would be so much easier if Max could go with her. She'd thought about it over and over, how she could make it work. But every time she tried to put her father with Max, Max with her father, all she saw was pain and hurt, on all sides.

Merry Christmas.

''Why aren't all these people at home? Drinking egg nog and cooing over darned mittens?''

''I need to call him.''

Max glanced at her. ''What?''

''My father. I don't know where he is. I need him there so we can talk.'' She pulled the cell phone out of her purse, wondering if she had any battery left. It came on, but the conversation would have to be short. She dialed the house. After four rings the machine answered. It was her voice.

''Dad? Are you there? It's me. Pick up.''

But he didn't. She hung up, and dialed his cell phone. Where would he be on Christmas? He should be home, with her, opening gifts, remembering Mom. Eating goodies and complaining that he had to go to the British Embassy for a fancy dinner, when all he wanted was to stay home with his girl.

''Hello?''

''Dad?''

There was a long silence. She heard faint music, a Christmas carol, but nothing else that would tell her where he was, what he was doing.

''Baby?''

She wiped her eyes as she nodded. ''It's me, Dad. Where are you?''

"Me? I'm… Where are you? Oh, my God."

She listened to him cry, and it was the first time she'd heard the sound since the day her mother died. "Dad, I'm going home. I'm on my way now. Meet me there, okay? Now?"

"Yes, yes. I'll be there, too. Half an hour."

"I'll be there. Just, don't say anything to anyone, okay? Don't tell."

"Yes, okay. Yes. Oh, Jade. God, you're alive."

"Yes, Daddy. I'm alive. I'm fine. I just miss you."

He didn't respond. She didn't think he could.

"I'm going to hang up now. But I'll see you soon." She pressed the button, and the connection was lost.

Max touched her shoulder. She laid her cheek on his hand, taking comfort, knowing it was the last time. And she cried.

"WHAT ABOUT SECURITY?"

They had driven around the block before heading into the driveway of her father's old colonial home. Just seeing the familiar yard, covered in snow, with the wreath she'd put on the door, made Jade want to turn the car around and go back to the cabin. "Drive around back," she said. "There's enough room for the car. It used to be a greenhouse, but we took it out after my mother died." She looked back at the front of the house. "I don't think he's home yet. There aren't any lights on."

Although it was mid-afternoon, the sky was overcast. Most of the houses on the high-end street were lit up, and not just on the outside. She'd seen silhouettes, people moving about, families. "I'll come out as soon as I can. But I want to prepare him. Give him a chance to… You know.''

Max nodded. ''I'll wait.''

She kissed him, lingering, breathing in his scent.

He was the one who pulled back. It wasn't to ask her to leave, but to plead with her to stay. Not that he said a word. His eyes, however, were eloquent.

''We'll get through this,'' she said. Then before she started crying again, she got out into the frigid air. She didn't bother bringing a thing with her, except for her purse and the tape. That, she stuck in her jacket pocket.

The walk to the front door took all her strength, and it was a relief to find herself alone. That wouldn't last for long, and there was something she wanted to do now, before her father arrived.

She went to his office. When she turned on the light, everything was at once familiar and completely foreign. She recognized every piece of furniture, all the books, his big oak desk and the worn leather chairs. The pictures on the bookshelf of her, her mother, the whole family at different stages, put a lump in her throat. It was good that she had to get this done, now.

His computer turned on with the flick of a button on the power strip. After it booted, she went into his private files, crossing her fingers that he hadn't changed the password. He hadn't. It was her mother's middle name. Ruth.

It didn't take her long to find what she was looking for. A bank account. The amounts were stunning, and she knew he could never have accumulated so much liquidity without seriously compromising his future.

Or by gambling. She knew which one it was. God, her heart felt so heavy, like it was made of stone.

She sat in the chair, staring at a paper clip, until she heard him open the front door. When his footsteps echoed in the hall outside, she stood up. Screw it, she couldn't stop crying. Which was okay, because he was crying, too.

They met by the door, and she was wrapped in his arms, the familiar scent of his aftershave smelling like home. He couldn't stop hugging her, making it a bit difficult to breathe. When he finally let her go, his tears flowed freely down his face, which looked oh, so old. It was as if he'd aged ten years. His hair was whiter, he'd missed a spot by his ear shaving, and his eyes were dark and hollow.

"I thought I'd lost you," he said.

"No, I'm here. And I'll be here. I promise. No matter what."

Her father didn't seem to hear. He just stared at her, confused for a long moment over her hair.

She touched her baseball cap with her hand. "We were hiding," she said.

"Did he hurt you? I swear by all that's holy, I'll find that bastard and I'll make him pay. I won't stop until he's in jail. Until he suffers—"

"Dad, please, stop. It's not Max's fault."

Her father stepped back, his eyes shocked and hurt. "Not his fault? He kidnapped my baby, and it's not his fault? He's hypnotized you, tricked you. But don't worry. You're home now. We'll get you to a doctor. We should call now, take you to the hospital."

"No. We have to talk."

"Later. There'll be time for that—"

"Dad, stop." She raised her voice, trying to pierce through his panic. "Stop!"

He took hold of her shoulders. "I insist you see a doctor. God knows what that pervert did to you. I swear, I'll kill him with my own hands—"

"Dad, I know. About everything."

His fingers tightened, hurting her, but his expression only got more confused.

"About Geotech, the *Irish Mist.* The bank account. I know you didn't have anything to do with the death of Werner Edwards, but I do know you've made sure Geotech will get the contract. That you had to."

Whatever color he had drained away, and she was left staring at the ghost of her father. "What are you talking about?"

"It's over. You don't have to lie anymore. I know, it's going to be terrible, but it'll end, if you do what you have to. I'll be here. I'll be by your side—"

He stepped back, letting her go as if touching her burned. "He lied to you. He made it all up. Framed me. You know that. You know me. You know what I stand for. Who I am."

"And I know Mom's death nearly killed you."

"Don't. Don't talk about her."

Jade stepped toward him, but he backed away. It was like speaking to a frightened child, and she was getting pretty damn scared herself. "You got lost, Dad, that's all. You were sick. People will understand."

"Understand that he corrupted you? That he twisted everything around, and made me the scapegoat?"

His voice had gotten high and shrill, his eyes wild.

She put out her hand, and he winced, as if she was going to strike him. "I saw, Daddy," she said, lowering her voice, making sure not to make any quick movements. "I saw a tape. They taped you when you were on the boat. Tricked you."

"No. I was never on a boat. There are no tapes!"

She slowly unzipped her jacket, and pulled out the cassette. "It's all here, Dad. And if they had copies on the boat, they have them elsewhere. Geotech is blackmailing you, I know that. They cheated and got you to lose so much money."

"No."

She nodded. Dying for him. "We have to do the right thing. Now, before anything else bad happens. Two people have died, Dad, and I know you don't want that. More will die if we don't stop this."

He shook his head, still in such denial she wasn't sure what she'd have to do.

When she went up to him, he didn't back away, although she could tell it was a struggle. She took his hand in hers and led him, calmly, around his desk. "I found the account, Daddy. It's all there, in black and white."

"No," he said, his voice so quiet it was barely a whisper.

"We can get through this. Together. I won't leave you. I'll stay here. Live here. And we'll do whatever we have to, to make sure Geotech is taken down."

He walked backward, staring from her to the computer screen and back again. Finally, he hit the bookshelf at the far end of the room. Only he didn't stop. Instead, he stepped, quickly, to his left and opened the liquor cabinet door. It wasn't until he turned back to her that she saw the gun.

"Dad, no!"

His hand shook as if he was palsied. It rose, trembling, until the barrel was halfway to his head.

Fear crippled her for a moment, where she couldn't speak or scream. She wanted Max. Max was just outside and he would know what to do. He would stop her father.

And because there was a God, her prayer was answered. The door behind her opened.

She turned, relief flooding her down to her toes.

Only it wasn't Max.

MAX MOVED ACROSS the distance from his car to the rear window of the house. The light had been on for a long time, but he'd waited, wanting Jade to come out, to tell him she'd talked to her dad. Only, he'd heard a car. A second car.

The first had been the senator's. Max had gone into the snow to make sure, and he'd watched the older man make his way into the house. Even from a distance, Max could see he'd aged years in just a few weeks. The guilt had to be killing him.

The second car had startled him, and once again he'd gone out and crept through the snow. He wasn't in time to see who'd gone in the house, but he did see that no other lights in the house went on. Keeping as close to the side of the building as he could, he made his way back to the rear window. Something was wrong. He knew it as well as he knew he'd do whatever it took to make sure Jade was safe.

"YOU," PARKER said behind her.

Jade took two steps to her left, to get between her father and Retik. Retik's gun.

"Well, how very convenient," the man said, showing his silver tooth as he smiled. "The papers will have a field day. Murder-suicide with such a famous player."

"What do you want?" her father asked, and she knew he had to be in shock, because there was absolutely no doubt. He wanted them dead, the evidence destroyed.

Her prayer, however useless, changed, willing Max to stay away. Get as far as he could from this house, this sickening ending.

"But you're lucky, Senator," Retik said. "You won't have to watch your daughter die."

"Don't hurt her."

Retik shook his head. She wondered, stupidly, why he had the tooth. He was such an ordinary man, in his line of business, he could have blended in with everyone else, been impossible to trace. But maybe that was the point. Maybe he wanted his victims to know who he was. "There's only one way to save her, Senator. If you're a good boy, and you put that muzzle right into your mouth, and pull the trigger, then I'll let her go."

"He's lying," Jade said, afraid to turn around, to let Retik out of her sight.

"Perhaps, but it is your only chance. Face it. Your father's already dead. Even if he doesn't die here, now, he's going to be murdered by the press. Crucified by the masses. And we all know what a proud man he is, don't we?"

''People know about you, Retik, and they know about Geotech. The evidence is out there. If you kill us, it'll just make things worse.''

He laughed. ''Worse for whom? I'll collect my money and disappear. I don't give a damn what happens to Geotech after my contract is out. But this is getting boring. Do it, old man. Kill yourself now, and save yourself the pain.''

''I won't. Not until you let her go.''

Retik sighed. ''Very well—''

Jade ducked, ran to the desk. ''Shoot him, Dad! Shoot him.''

Retik shook his head and aimed at her father's heart, not even bothering to hurry. When she looked back at her father, he was frozen still, the gun wasn't shaking any longer. But it wasn't pointed at Retik.

A crash, so loud, she screamed, came from the window in front of her. She ducked her head, but saw that Retik had spun around at the sound.

And there was Max, and he was charging like a bull, yelling his head off. She didn't wait. She ran to her father, yanking the weapon from his hand, turning to point it at the killer. But he was on his back, on the floor, and Max was on top of him, and they were struggling, both of them holding Retik's gun.

Her heart hammered so hard in her chest she thought she would die. ''Max, I've got him. Get away!''

But Max, his face red with strain, couldn't get away, and the gun was moving inexorably closer to firing position. If she didn't do something, he was going to die. They were all going to die.

She let her breath go and raised her gun, aiming as

carefully as she knew how, praying that she wouldn't shake, that she would kill the right man.

And then she pulled the trigger.

THE EXPLOSION deafened him, and for a long moment, the torture of the struggle continued, him pushing, pushing. Until there was nothing to push against. Retik's hand flew back, hitting him in the face. Max fell forward, collapsing on the still body.

He wanted to move, to get the hell away, but his legs wouldn't obey, his arms were frozen. Until he heard Jade call his name.

He rolled over, landing with his back on the Persian carpet. He wasn't shot. Of that he was quite sure. But he had to make sure Retik was.

Scrambling to his feet, he kicked Retik's weapon across the floor, then his own. Only then did he see that Retik wasn't going anywhere. The back of his head was gone.

He turned to Jade, who still had her gun in both hands. Tears flowed down her cheeks, and her whole body trembled. He barely noticed the pale man behind her as he rushed to her side, slipped the gun from her fingers. Wrapped her in his arms. "It's over," he said, rocking her, holding her as tightly as he could. "He's dead, it's over."

Jade melted against him and he held her up, let her cry, smelled the acrid smoke from the gun, but beneath that was her scent, the sweet apple from her shampoo. His hands touched her back, her neck, her arms, just making sure that nothing was wrong, that she was whole and okay.

He closed his eyes, so grateful he barely knew how to think. Thank God he'd heard Retik's car.

After a long while, he couldn't say how long, she stood on her own, pulled back from his embrace. For a moment, he thought she was going to kiss him, but she didn't. She stepped away, out of his arms. Walked to her father.

She touched his cheek with the palm of her hand. "Daddy," she said.

The man collapsed, his shoulders folding, his head bent in shame and fear and shock. Jade held him, helped him to the big leather wing chair in the center of the room.

"I'm sorry," the senator said, over and over and over.

Jade didn't respond, except to say, "Shh," as she touched him, soothed him. Her father buried his head in his hands and wept.

Without turning, Jade said, "Max, please call 911."

He went to the phone, found out he wasn't too steady himself as he punched in the three numbers. A moment later, he reported a shooting. Jade supplied him with the address.

Then it was all a blur. Police, FBI, a crowd outside. He didn't even get to say goodbye to Jade. He was up for thirty-one hours straight, answering questions, showing his evidence. Peter came, and they questioned him, too.

When he asked what was happening with the senator, with Jade, they wouldn't tell him.

He didn't care a damn about his story. Didn't even

care that his father had come, with an attorney in tow, and that he'd had to slog through the legal B.S.

He just missed her. Missed whatever chance they could have had. Should have had.

He'd won, but the loss was so great, it nearly killed him.

Chapter Fifteen

Six months later…

Jade finished putting the dishes away and closed the cupboard. Her gaze moved to the mirror above the sink, and she was startled again at how her face had changed. There were tiny lines by her eyes, by the edges of her mouth. Her hair, back to her natural auburn, was short now. She had no time or desire to do much with it.

But why shouldn't she look different? Her whole world had gone insane. She couldn't remember the last time she'd laughed. When her father wasn't constantly on her mind. The Senate hearings were still going on. He'd lost his seat, and they wouldn't know for a long time what the ultimate outcome would be. He was guilty, yes. But his sentence could be anything from probation to years in prison.

It would kill him, if they locked him up. Already, he was a shadow of the man he'd been. Disgraced, maligned, vilified. Some, who knew better, sympathized with his downfall, remembered who he had been, but the public, with their short memories, had written him off as another politician gone bad.

He'd already had one heart attack. It had been mild, but also a warning. She did her best to protect him, but it was difficult. The hardest thing of all, for him, was the humiliation.

He'd come completely clean. Geotech was in the headlines daily now, their government contract canceled, and C. J. Harris was going down, hard.

Max, of course, had written it all. Told all the dirty little secrets, given the evidence that had put the final nail in the coffin. He'd been as compassionate as possible about her father, but what could he do? The truth was the truth.

If only she could stop thinking about him. Missing him was a physical thing, an ache that nothing could assuage. Seeing his byline, even hearing him on the radio, was a knife, twisting in her heart.

There was nothing to be done. She'd told them all about how he'd known the truth from the beginning. They'd tried to get her to press charges on the kidnapping, but not for long. She'd painted him for the hero he was, and his words about her made her cry herself to sleep. When she slept.

Mostly, she remembered. The fear, yes, but that wasn't the important thing. His kindness. His touch. The way he made her body come alive.

"Jade."

"I'll be right there, Dad."

She turned off the light in the kitchen, and went to the den. Her father didn't go to his library much anymore. Mostly, he watched old movies. His concentration still wasn't great, but not because he didn't try.

The weight of his crimes was too heavy, making him seem so very small.

"What's up, Dad? Can I get you some tea?"

He shook his head. Smiled at her. "You know what I thought about this morning?" he asked.

"What?"

"That I never did give you a Christmas present."

She sighed. "It's okay. We were a little busy."

He held his hand out to her. "I want to give you something. For all you've done. For being the daughter you are."

She held his hand, leaned over and kissed his dry cheek. "I love you."

"And I love you. The only thing that matters to me now is your happiness."

Jade smiled tightly. She knew he meant it, but that the one thing that would make her happy, if she even could be happy seeing him like this, was something she could never have.

"I'm ashamed that through all my troubles, I didn't put your happiness first," her father said, his voice older, more enfeebled. "I was selfish. I let the loss of your mother cripple the most important parts of me. But nothing hurts more than that I hurt you. That I continue to hurt you. I know you've put your studies on hold. That you've given up so much of your life because of my mistakes."

"Dad, please. You'd do the same for me. We're family. We stick together."

"But I'm not the only family you should have. You're a beautiful woman, Jade. With so much to offer. You've never done anything but make me proud."

Tears came, and even as she wiped the traces away from her cheeks, more fell. She felt so powerless. Watching him so humble, so full of pain, filled her with anger and grief.

"The Christmas present I never gave you," he said, his gaze moving back to the clock on his desk. "I want to give it to you now."

She looked around the office. Seeing no package, her gaze went back to her father.

The doorbell rang. She stood, cross that the press people would bother them so late. Either that, or someone from the Senate. They didn't give a damn that her father needed his rest.

"Go get the door," he said.

"Let them wait until tomorrow."

"No, honey." He smiled, but there was a hint of sadness in his eyes. Of course, she'd come to expect that. "It's your present."

Confused, she let him go, and headed through the house to the front door. She hesitated for a moment, thinking it must be flowers, but no one delivered this late at night. She turned the knob, and swung the door open.

What she saw took her breath.

"Hey," Max said.

She just stood there, mouth open, eyes wide, the damn tears coming again full force. It was really him. With his dark hair back, wearing clothes she'd never seen, a bunch of roses in his hand. Max.

"Oh, the hell with this," he said, and then he was inside, and she was in his arms. She kissed him, or he kissed her, it didn't matter, because it was him, and she held him so tight he probably couldn't breathe.

He tasted the same, smelled a little better, felt like all her dreams come true. He kissed her nose and her cheeks and her chin, and she heard herself laughing.

And then he kissed her again, and he kicked the door shut behind them. "I missed you so much," he said, his breath touching hers. "Every day, every minute. It killed me not to call you, or talk to you."

"Oh, God, yes," she said. She pulled back, holding his head steady between her hands. "I don't understand."

He smiled. "Your dad called me this afternoon. He told me I'd better come, because his little girl was in love. And he never wanted to hurt her again."

She laughed. And cried. And she would never let him go.